The Secret Theatre

Luke Temple

IndePenPress

www.thistlewick.net
www.luketemple.co.uk

First published in Great Britain by Indepenpress

All paper used in the printing of this book has been made
from wood grown in managed, sustainable forests.

ISBN13: 978-1-907172-93-9

Printed and bound in the UK
Indepenpress is an imprint of Indepenpress Publishing Limited
25 Eastern Place
Brighton
BN2 1GJ

A catalogue record of this book is available from
the British Library

Cover, illustrations and stray cat font by Jessica Chiba

The Secret Theatre

Dear Emily,

With best wishes,

Luke

March
2014

 # A Story from Thistlewick Island

Book 2

Welcome to Thistlewick Island, which was established in 1712 by Lord Samuel Lewis Thistlewick. The kind and gallant Lord Thistlewick set the island up as a farming community, and since then it has grown, quite slowly, to become an independent island. The people who now inhabit Thistlewick (or Thistlewickians as they call themselves) are peaceful and friendly. Everyone knows each other and they pride themselves on living completely separately from the rest of the world.

The children who grow up here have great freedom to play around most parts of the island. But there are some areas that they are forbidden from going near, because, for all its niceties, Thistlewick Island also holds many dark secrets, which have left some islanders superstitious and scared.

On the whole, though, Thistlewick is an extraordinarily beautiful place to live, with lush greenery, quaint cottages and some wonderful wildlife. No matter where you are on the island, you can always hear the hum of the majestic blue sea.

Previous books in the 'Thistlewick Island' series:
Book 1 – 'Stormy Cliff'

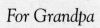

For Grandpa

3rd January 1953

Bang! Bang! Bang!

Three clear, repetitive hits. The noise travelled all the way from the front door down to where Emily sat, perfectly still, holding the diary in her hands.

She would have been scared before, but now she was prepared. She had been preparing herself for the last two days, for she had known this was going to happen.

Bang! Bang! Bang!

How does the noise reach me so clearly? she thought.

She was a long way from the front door. The banging only acted to remind her just how powerful *they* were.

And how powerful she would have to be. She knew she wouldn't win against them – one of her and... what... ten of them? Would they deem ten a big enough number to deal with one defenceless woman? But she would fight them. She would fight them with her whole life for everything she believed in, to the end.

She calmly finished writing the final entry in the diary, closed it and placed it carefully down next to her. Then she studied her surroundings for the final time, the beautiful reds and golds. She hoped so much that *they* wouldn't find it.

'Goodbye,' she said to the room around her. And the room replied, bouncing the soft echo of her voice back to her.

Emily climbed down from the stage, took a deep breath, and walked towards the door. As she went, a smile appeared on her face, a determined smile. The smile of a person who knew their fate and was ready to embrace it.

And then she walked out to greet *them*.

Part 1

CHAPTER 1

An Unknown Address

Rebecca Evans squinted at the envelope. The scratchy writing was hard to read.

'Mr... Mr R Sharpe, Stall four... no, five, Market Square, Thistlewick.'

She finally managed to make sense of the address and dropped the letter into an empty space on the floor. She picked up another one.

Rebecca, or Becky as she preferred to be known, lived on Thistlewick Island. The close-knit community of Thistlewick existed completely independently from the rest of the world. The island had its own laws and currency, its own farms and fishing fleet, its own shops and its very own post office. This was where Becky sat now, in the sorting room amongst various piles of scattered letters and packages.

'Ted Castle, The Harbour, Thistlewick.'

She found the rest of the letters going to the harbour, added this new one to the pile and tied them all tightly together with string. She had been repeating this process for what felt like several hours now.

Why do I have to do this on the first day of the summer holidays? Becky thought. She really wanted to be outside playing with her best friend, Jimmy, in the sun, rather than sitting in this small, windowless room.

The Thistlewick post mistress was known to the islanders as 'Postie Babs', and to Becky as Mum. It was at this time of year, early in the summer, that the postal service became busiest. Becky's mum couldn't sort through the post on her own, and so each year Becky and her older brother William helped her out.

On this particular day, though, William was messing about in the garden of his two best friends, the twins Ben and Harriet Davies, helping them to build a tree house. This left Becky on her own in the sorting room, sifting through more post than she had ever encountered before, while Postie Babs served customers in the shop.

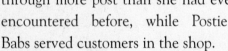

Why does Will get to see his friends and I don't?

Becky glared down at the official looking letter she was holding.

'Mrs S Price, three Village Green, Thistlewick.'

More string.

'Mr C Silverdale, The White Wing Pub and Hotel, Thistlewick.'

More string, and some tape to seal up the tear in that letter.

Becky was small as eleven-year-olds went. She wore her long chestnut hair loosely and had bright blue eyes that matched her personality. Her brother swore he'd seen them glow in the dark when she went to bed, but she had pointed out that he couldn't have seen this, because when she was in bed her eyes were closed. William was just jealous, because he had inherited dull brown eyes from their mum.

Becky searched around on the floor for something more interesting than a letter, and picked up a large brown parcel.

She sat up and reread the address. She didn't recognise the name of the house or the occupant.

'That's really strange,' she said. Thistlewick was only small, and she thought she knew what every house on the island was called.

'Everything alright, love?' Becky's mum had popped her head around the door. She looked red-faced and flustered. 'Why that old woman, Gladys, insists on paying for everything in one pence pieces I don't know. She stood there for a whole ten minutes counting out three pounds eighty four while a huge queue built up behind her.'

'Mum, I think this parcel's been sent to the wrong island.'

'Oh, why's that?' Her mum walked into the room.

'I don't recognise the address at all.'

'Pass it here, love.'

Becky stood up and handed her mum the parcel. They both stared at the address, and a thoughtful look appeared on Becky's mum's face.

'Well, that is interesting,' she said. 'There hasn't been anything sent to Midsummer House since... well, since before you or I were born.'

'So it is on Thistlewick then?' Becky asked.

'Oh yes, this house is on the east side of the island. It's been in terrible ruins for years – as long as I can remember. No one lives there.'

'So who is Emily Wilson?' Becky pointed to the name in the address.

'I have no idea. I don't think I've ever heard of her. Hmmm...'

A bell rang in the shop and Becky's mum looked away from the parcel. Becky knew she had lost interest in it, just at the point it was getting *more* interesting. Her mum handed the brown object back to Becky and turned around to leave.

'It's probably best just to throw it in the bin,' she said.

'But if it's addressed to a house that still exists we should deliver it, shouldn't we?'

'Oh, Becky, I don't know…' The ringing came from the shop again. Her mum sighed. 'Look, I've got customers to deal with. You can deliver the parcel if you really want to.'

Becky grinned – finally, she had an excuse to get outside and go exploring.

'But Becky, just deliver the parcel and then walk straight away from the house,' her mum warned in her most forceful voice. '*No* trying to find adventures. I know what you're like.'

CHAPTER 2
Midsummer House

It was true, Becky's mum did know what she was like. She had always been a bit of an adventurer, ever since she was three and had tried to climb up the chimney to find Father Christmas, only to land back down in the fireplace covered in black soot, with a bemused smile on her face.

Becky knew what she was like too, and secretly always looked for new things to explore. She had been really jealous when, the previous year, Ben and Harriet had been sent on a dangerous mission to find treasure to save Stormy Cliff School.

I wish that had been me, she'd thought many times.

Anyway, now she had finished sorting through all the post at the post office, she walked out into the bright afternoon sunlight, with the parcel addressed to Midsummer House held tightly in her hands.

It's not the most exciting thing, but this is still an adventure, she told herself, *I've got a house to find, which Mum says is rundown and abandoned.*

A small smile appeared on her face.

The post office was situated in the Market Square, a collection of old, Tudor-style buildings at the centre of the island, which enclosed a variety of blue and red striped stalls.

At one of them the fisherman, Ted Castle, was busy laying out a display of particularly large fish. He was being helped by his son, Jack, who went to Stormy Cliff with Becky. They both waved at her as she walked past.

'Hello!' she called to them.

She looked over to Jimmy's house at the other side of the square and decided to ask if he wanted to come on her adventure.

Knocking on his red front door, she waited a few moments until a kindly-faced lady opened it, duster in hand.

'Hello, Becky,' said Jimmy's mum. 'Have you got some post for me, or is it Jimmy you're after?'

'No post today, Mrs Cole, but it would be great if Jimmy could come out.'

'Ok. He's just finished tidying his room, so I don't see why not.' She smiled at Becky. 'Jimmy! Becky's here!'

A few seconds later a neatly dressed, and very short, boy with shiny dark hair came bursting down the stairs, homemade model of a red space rocket in hand.

'Hi, Jimmy. I've got an adventure for us to go on.'

'Can I, Mum?' asked Jimmy.

'Go on,' she said, still smiling. 'You two go and have fun. Make sure you stay safe, though.'

'Come on, Jimmy!' Becky skipped away from the house.

Jimmy handed his mum the model rocket and jumped out through the front door after her.

The two children walked out of the Market Square, Becky in the lead with Jimmy close behind. As they headed east on a winding route, striding through the rolling grass and past the white houses with granite grey roofs, Becky showed her friend the parcel and told him about their mission.

'That sounds fun!' said Jimmy. 'So we just have to find this house and deliver the parcel?'

'Yep… and if the address says Forest Lane it must be somewhere near the forest, so we need to head straight up.'

At a fork in the path they changed direction onto a track that took them north.

The houses on Thistlewick were very spread out, with plenty of greenery between each one, and there weren't really any streets. This made the postal service a complicated skill to learn, Becky thought – when you delivered the post, the address on letters usually only gave the name of the house, so you had to know where on the island that house was in order to deliver the letter.

Jimmy always liked to test Becky's knowledge when they went walking.

'What's that one called?' he asked, pointing at a cosy looking place to their right.

'That's Sleepy Cottage, Jimmy, you can tell by the large sign on the door.'

'Oh. How about that one?' He pointed to his left at an unusually thin, pink house. 'That doesn't have a sign.'

'That's… um… that's Florence House.'

'See, I would never have known that. You must know the name of every building on Thistlewick.'

'Well, that's what I thought, until I found this parcel addressed to Emily Wilson at Midsummer House,' Becky pointed out.

Soon they had passed Treetops, the furthest away house that Becky knew of, and were coming close to the dark, twisted trees at the forest edge. When they reached the tall fence that stopped people getting into the forest, and other things getting out of it, they studied their surroundings.

'Which way should we go?' asked Jimmy.

Becky looked around. The nearest path would take them left, and back towards the market; but there was also a faint outline, which could once have been a path, heading right.

'Let's take this one,' she said, pointing along it.

'Are you sure? It doesn't look like it's been used much.'

'That's part of the fun, Jimmy. I bet you anything Midsummer House is this way. I'll race you!'

She shot off along the path, Jimmy stumbling along behind her.

Any sign of what might have been a path soon faded out, but they kept going, heading nearer to the eastern edge of the island. They hadn't passed any houses for quite a while.

'Are you sure we're going the right way?' called Jimmy.

'I don't know, but I haven't come this far just to turn back again. Come on!'

Then, a minute later, Becky saw it – the image of a large, square building, highlighted on the horizon.

'What a place! This must be it.'

***

Becky placed her hand on the rusty gate and carefully pushed. It gave way and slowly ached open, letting her walk through into a badly overgrown garden. Jimmy followed close behind her; Becky could tell he was getting a bit nervous.

Any tame plants that may once have lived in the garden had long been bullied out of the way by wild shrubs and nettles. Weeds lined the broken stone path and roots ran along it like dead snakes.

'You really have been abandoned,' Becky said to the garden.

The two children walked cautiously, avoiding stepping on anything odd-looking, and the wrecked house loomed tall in front of them. It was certainly grand, Becky thought – it might even have been beautiful once – but most of all it was big.

'Why have I never noticed this place before?' she said. 'I've been around the island enough times.'

'It's not somewhere we usually think about coming, is it?' replied Jimmy. 'I mean, this is the only building I can see around here.'

'That's true.' All that surrounded Midsummer House was flat grassland, and the forest on one side. The houses back in the main part of Thistlewick were like small specs on the horizon.

Staring up, Becky saw some parts of the house where the grey brickwork still held onto its peeling cream-painted cover. There were odd little touches around the garden too that showed the place might once have been cared for.

'Look at that wheelbarrow over there,' she said. 'That would have been nice to use.' But now the wooden object was full of stinging nettles, fighting for their place in the sun.

'And look,' said Jimmy, pointing in the other direction. 'A pond… All dried out now, though.'

Halfway up the path, hidden under a small tree Becky found a sign. As she cleared the branches from around it, she could just make out some cracked, artistic writing: 'Welcome to Midsummer House, home of Emily Wilson'.

'We've found it. This is definitely the place the parcel's addressed to.'

Becky walked up to the large oak front door, which was sheltered in a porch. She studied the rusty-looking letterbox and held the parcel up against it to size it up.

'There's no way it'll fit.'

'So what do we do now?' asked Jimmy.

'Follow post office regulations, I suppose. See if anyone's in.'

She breathed in deeply, took hold of the knocker and hit it three times against the door. The noise was loud and echoed for a long time through the house.

'If there's anyone there, they'll definitely hear that.'

She waited several minutes, but there was no sound of movement.

'Can we go now?' Jimmy was starting to look uncomfortable.

'I suppose I could leave the parcel somewhere outside, or maybe I should take it back for Mum to throw away?'

As she stood debating what to do, she noticed the shining doorknob standing out from the darkness of the door. She had never seen one like it before – it had a sort of golden mask on it, with an inviting, smiley face. This made her mind up. Becky moved her hand around the doorknob. It turned.

The door swung open.

CHAPTER 3
The Secret Door

Becky peered in. Through the darkness and the dust she saw a tall hallway with doors to each side and a wide staircase leading upwards.

'Becky, what are you doing?' asked Jimmy. 'I don't think this is a good idea.'

She turned around to face him. 'I think we should go exploring.'

'Our mums wouldn't be very happy about that.'

'Well, I suppose Mum did tell me not to…' Becky looked through the entrance again – she couldn't help being drawn into it. 'But *your* Mum didn't tell us not to, did she? Anyway, no one needs to know.'

'I'm not sure about this…'

'We've got the chance to turn our small adventure into a much bigger one. There's a whole house to explore!'

Jimmy still looked doubtful.

'Well I'm going in even if you're not. You can follow me if you want to.' She stepped inside.

As her eyes became more accustomed to the low level of light she couldn't help but feel a bit disappointed. She didn't know quite what she'd expected to find inside – perhaps a hall lined with golden statues leading to a gigantic throne at the end, or maybe something creepier like a gruesome ghost chamber full of skeletons. But this hallway just felt empty, and smelt quite stale too. Still, the house was big and she was here to explore it. She moved towards the white marble staircase.

As she did she felt something brush against her.

'Decided to join me have you, Jimmy?'

She turned around, but in the darkness she couldn't see anyone there. There was another movement and she turned quickly around to see a dark figure in front of her.

'Jimmy?' she said, her voice starting to shake.

But it couldn't be Jimmy – this figure was at least a foot taller. And it was starting to move towards her!

'Yes?' the figure responded.

Then it became smaller, and as it got closer, Becky realised that it was Jimmy. He had just been standing on the first step of the staircase.

'Don't scare me like that!'

'I wasn't trying to scare you,' said Jimmy quietly. 'I'm scared enough as it is.'

'Well seeing as you're with me, let's start by going up there.'

'You can if you want. I'm not going any further than this first step.'

Becky set off up the staircase.

And came to her second disappointment. It was completely blocked off right at the top by a collection of large objects – broken chairs, a wardrobe and even a grandfather clock stopped her from getting to the first floor.

'This is annoying,' she called to Jimmy. 'Why is there a load of broken furniture piled up on a staircase? There's no way I can get past.'

She climbed down again, making loud, echoing footsteps on the hard surface as she went.

Becky now had four options – four doors that she could go through.

Well, five including the front door, but I'm not giving up yet.

She walked past Jimmy and over to the door immediately to her right, which was plain with a simple handle. It opened stiffly and she found a cupboard filled with even more furniture – tables this time, and a crumpled mattress with lots of holes in it. The second door on the right opened to reveal a small bathroom with a toilet that looked ancient, like the one at the church, which was over sixty years old.

She walked over to try the third door, on the other side of the hallway. This one had intricate markings carved around its edge, with swirls curling in various symmetrical patterns. There was also a word cut into the wood, in the same artistic lettering as the sign in the garden: Library.

'Now, this door has possibilities. Come and look, Jimmy.'

Jimmy edged over to her. 'A library. That doesn't look too scary.'

'I'm going to open the door,' she said.

'Ok.'

It glided open with ease, as if it had been used to opening and closing quite a lot, allowing Becky to peer into the room.

Two of its walls were completely covered from floor to ceiling with bookshelves; a third contained a large marble fireplace, and the wall opposite Becky had a tall window, which looked out over a magnificent view of the sea and the sky.

'A proper library,' she said.

As she moved into the room, Becky noticed there was no furniture – she assumed any that had once been here was crushed somewhere amongst the pile on the stairs, or in the cupboard. But she could imagine how wonderful it must have been to sit here in comfy chairs, enjoying the sea view or a warm fire in the evening.

'Finally, I've made a decent discovery! I told you Midsummer House was worth exploring.'

She glanced over at Jimmy. He was studying one of the bookshelves and his nervousness seemed to be easing slightly.

Becky began to search around the room, keen to find anything that might tell her more about the house, or Emily Wilson.

On the mantelpiece above the fire she spied a collection of silver photo frames. She went over and picked up the smallest one, which was circular and had a thin crack running through it. The black and white photo inside was very faded from its years of exposure to the  sun, but showed a beautiful woman in her thirties, her eyes and smile alive.

'Are you Emily Wilson?'

 The photo behind it was bigger, in a rectangular frame, and showed a group of fifteen people, formally arranged but dressed in a strange array of outfits. Several elderly men were dressed up as knights; a grinning boy in a sailor's outfit stood at the front, and there was the woman from the previous photo wearing a long flowing gown and with the same shining eyes and smile. She was hugging the sailor boy tightly.

'Look at this, Jimmy.'

Jimmy walked over, a big book in his hand.

'Why are they all dressed so funnily?' he asked.

'I don't know, but that boy in the sailor's outfit looks just like you.'

'Does he?'

'Yeah, except he's bigger, of course!'

'Oi!'

'What's that book you've got about?'

'It's a story called *Outer Space: A Thistlewick Warlock's Prediction* and it's about going into space!'

'I could have guessed that. Sounds like your sort of book.'

Jimmy moved away and sat down on the floor under the windowsill, opening the book to the first page. Becky turned back to the mantelpiece.

Most of the other photos were of various landscapes around Thistlewick, all in black and white. One showed the Market Square, and Becky saw the post office in the corner – it looked pretty much the same as it was today. There was a date on the photo – 1951.

'So Midsummer House must have been lived in last in the nineteen fifties, according to this photo anyway. That's about... sixty years ago,' she calculated, turning around to Jimmy. But he was too engrossed in his book to notice.

Why is the house in such a bad state? she wondered. *What happened to Emily Wilson? Why doesn't she live here now?*

She moved over to the bookshelves. There must have been thousands of books, but Becky decided to scan along the ones at her eye-level, about four shelves up, reading the titles on their thick spines: *A Guide To Island Gardens*; *Medieval Fashion*; *The Life and Times of Wally Winterbottom*. They were all very big and old-fashioned, and didn't seem to be in any particular order. It was incredible that Jimmy had managed to find a book about space so quickly.

She pulled *Thistlewick: A History* off the shelf, but put it back when she saw how much writing was on each page.

About halfway along the shelf, she came to a book called *Theatre: A Beginner's Guide*. The word 'Theatre' caught her attention. Becky remembered seeing a place called a theatre on the mainland – a grand old building with lots of pillars in front of it – but she'd never been allowed near it, which had left her curious as to what was inside.

She placed her hand on the book to pull it out. But when she tried, the book only came out halfway and got stuck.

'Come on!'

She pulled again, harder.

There was a loud click and Becky jumped back. The bookcase suddenly slid sideways and disappeared!

In the space it left was a door in the wall. Becky stared, open-mouthed.

'Wow! A secret door.'

The noise of the bookcase moving had caused Jimmy to look up. 'What… what happened?'

But Becky didn't really hear Jimmy. She moved towards the door, her hand outstretched. The doorknob that stood out from it was identical to the one on the front door – a golden mask with a smiley face. Her heart started to beat faster, and her hand shook slightly as it moved towards the doorknob.

She looked back at Jimmy. 'You coming?'

'Er… a secret door. I don't think so. There could be anything in there…'

***

As she stepped through the doorway, Becky was greeted by total darkness. She couldn't see a thing.

She heard the door closing behind her and panicked. She turned around to hurry out again – she'd gone too far this time. But before she reached the door, it snapped shut.

Oh no, I'm trapped!

Shaking, Becky tumbled forwards in the pitch black, trying to find a way out. She hit her knee on something very hard and let out a cry of pain. The sound echoed eerily all around her.

Where am I?

Then, as if by magic, her question was answered and the room was filled with light.

CHAPTER 4
The Red Room

A sea of rich red and golden colours flowed out in front of her, splashing around every corner of the room, lapping up the walls and filling her mind with an incredibly beautiful vision. Becky's eyes opened wide and she felt breathless. It was a while before she could take in all the detail.

Rows and rows of plush red seats stretched out along an equally red carpet, all pointing in the same direction, to a raised platform far above them. This was clearly the centre of attention. A huge red curtain, the biggest Becky had ever seen, was stretched between two golden pillars at the back of the platform.

At the top-most point of the ceiling was one of the golden masks with a smiley face, at least as tall as Becky's whole body and shining brilliantly. Next to it was another mask, but this one had a sad-looking face.

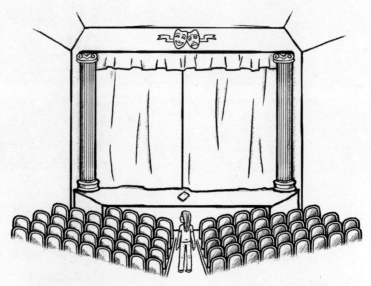

I wonder what they're for. They must be important.

As Becky moved forwards, she realised she had been standing under a sort of balcony, which covered half of the room and had lots more seats on it, all placed to face the raised platform at the front.

What is this room meant to be used for? It's so different from all the other rooms in the house.

Nothing like it had ever been seen on Thistlewick before, Becky was sure.

I must be the first person to discover it, she thought.

As she finally reached the platform, she found steps leading up to it. She climbed them and stood in front of the curtain, looking out over the ocean of seats below. This was clearly a place meant for a large audience. Becky tried to picture people filling all the seats, but she couldn't. The nearest thing to this on the island was the school hall, and that could only seat fifty people at once. This room could hold at least five times that amount.

But why is it hidden behind a bookcase?

She tried speaking. 'Hello!'

Her voice echoed strongly around, reaching every seat, bouncing around the walls and coming back to her as if the room itself had spoken. She felt powerful standing up on the platform looking out, as if she had control of the whole room.

She moved forwards to the edge of the platform, and nearly tripped over. Balancing herself, she looked down. Lying at her feet was a small book. Its leather cover was of the same grand red colour as the seats below her, and it lay there as if challenging her to pick it up.

She did.

It looked similar to the books from years gone by that were kept at Thistlewick Church, so it must have been old. But unlike the books at the Church it was in perfect condition, without a single scuffmark, crease or bend.

Becky turned the book around in her hands. There was no writing on the cover to reveal what it contained, and so, hands trembling, she opened it to the first page. There were nine words, tidy and welcoming, just like the writing on the sign outside and the library door. They read:

'The Diary of the Secret Theatre
by Emily Wilson'

CHAPTER 5

Banned!

'Mum! Mum!'

Becky had stopped only briefly to tell Jimmy about what she'd found and then ran straight home. She'd made the discovery of her life, and surely the greatest discovery in the history of Thistlewick. She, Becky Evans, had found the Secret Theatre!

'What is it, love?' said her mum, clearly surprised by Becky's sudden entrance into their house above the post office. She turned around from her position at the kitchen sink, where she was peeling potatoes.

'You won't believe what I've found!' Becky shrieked from the doorway.

She stood, practically bouncing up and down, still holding the parcel, behind which she had hidden the diary.

Her mum glanced at her suspiciously. 'Usually when you say something like that, it means you've been doing things you shouldn't have. This isn't another chimney moment, is it?'

Her mum called all of Becky's attempts at adventure her 'chimney moments'.

'No, Mum, this is proper. This is *much* bigger.'

'Go on then, spill the beans. Oh, and pass me another potato.'

Becky grabbed one of the large brown potatoes from the wicker basket behind the door and threw it to her mum, frustrated that she was carrying on with what she was doing, and not devoting her full attention to what Becky had to say.

'I've found a theatre!'

Catching the potato, Barbara Evans frowned. 'A what?'

'It's this huge room with hundreds of seats all covered in red and there's a big platform at the front and two golden masks, one has a happy face and the other has a sad face.'

'Slow down, love. What are you talking about? Hang on, theatre…'

Becky's mum stared thoughtfully at the potato, then her eyebrows rose as if she had just remembered what a theatre was. Becky looked at her eagerly.

'No, that's impossible. It's not like you to make things up, Becky, and I don't know why you are now.'

Becky opened her mouth and closed it again. She was stunned.

'How did you find out about theatre anyway?' her mum continued. 'You can't have learnt about it at school.'

'I… well…' Becky couldn't speak. *Why doesn't she believe me?*

'Where have you really been?'

'Midsummer House.'

Her mum looked at the parcel in Becky's hand.

'Let me guess.' Her voice rose slightly. 'You knocked on the door but there was no reply, so… so you took it upon yourself to enter the house?'

Becky's eyes fell. 'Yes.'

Her mum dropped the potato into the sink with a loud thud and moved towards her, waving the peeler threateningly.

'I specifically told you not to do that! Midsummer House is dangerous, very dangerous. No one's been near it for years. It could have collapsed on top of you! But no, you think that breaking in and having a nose around is perfectly fine. You have more right than anyone else, do you? That place is deserted for a reason, you know. I cannot believe you!'

'But I went with Jimmy and…'

'You dragged poor Jimmy along too? I don't want to hear it Rebecca.'

Becky knew it hadn't been right of her to go into Midsummer House, but she hadn't broken in, the door had been unlocked, and she had found the Secret Theatre. Surely that outweighed her wrongdoing?

'But the theatre—' she pleaded.

'It's impossible for there to be a theatre!' her mother shouted.

'Why?'

'Because theatre was banned on Thistlewick over fifty years ago!'

Becky couldn't stop her mouth from falling open. Her mind suddenly became a landslide, and all her thoughts tumbled sharply down, back to reality. Less than an hour ago she had discovered a theatre, the most wonderful place she had ever seen, and now her mother had dropped a bombshell right on top of it.

But it has to be real, doesn't it? I was there, I stood inside it!

She felt the diary clutched in her hand, behind the parcel, and was desperate to read it to prove to herself that she hadn't imagined the last few hours.

'At seven o'clock, we will take that parcel to the Thistlewick Council meeting. They can decide what to do with it,' her mother said slowly. 'Now, I would like you to go to your room.'

Good, Becky thought.

***

Theatres have been banned on Thistlewick?

Becky dropped the parcel onto her bedside cabinet and stared at the diary. It was definitely real – that royal-red cover – and so was the theatre. So why hadn't her mother believed her? Why had she said theatres were banned?

Becky hadn't been sure if she wanted to show the diary to her mother yet, but after the argument they'd just had, she wasn't even going to tell her about it.

I'll find someone else who'll believe me!

She slumped down onto her bed and stared angrily ahead.

Becky's bedroom was small and tucked away in one corner of the house. The part of the ceiling above her bed slanted downwards with the shape of the roof and a series of oak beams stretched across it. The window beside her bed was open, and a warm, gentle breeze blew in from the sea and began to calm her.

She opened the diary again to the first page. *The Secret Theatre*. Perhaps her mum was right and theatres *were* banned on Thistlewick; that would explain why this was a secret one.

Why would a theatre be banned, though? It's such an amazing place.

But then, Becky realised, she didn't even know what was meant to happen in a theatre. She turned over to the next page and began to read the words of Emily Wilson.

July 27th 1952

Welcome to the diary of the Secret Theatre, which is located at Midsummer House, my home and, I'm told, the perfect place for a theatre.

Today marks a very special event. We have been planning out the theatre for some time to see if it would be possible.

The fantastic news: it is! And today we officially start building it!

I will get onto who the 'we' are (a wonderful group of people) and also why we are building a 'secret' theatre, in future entries.

First, though, I feel I ought to tell you about what theatre is. Who knows, by the time you come to read this, theatre may have been forgotten and you won't have a clue what I'm talking about. I hope with all my heart that this isn't the case, for I cannot imagine a life without theatre. That is why the Secret Theatre is so important. It is our fight against 'them'!

I will get onto who 'they' are later as well — I want to focus on happy things now, on this marvellous day. The sad part of it all can come later.

So: theatre! My love, my joy, my passion! I will give you the most general definition I can in this entry, but it's hard, for I could talk about it forever.

Theatre basically has two meanings. The first is the room where the second takes place, if that makes sense. It doesn't have to be a specific room, it could simply be a field or a church hall — we have used both of these as our theatres for many years. At the most basic level there's a stage for the performers and a seating area for an audience. The most impressive room, though, is one dedicated entirely to theatre, and this is what the Secret Theatre will be. I have given you no indication of how amazing theatres are, but for now I will say that theatres are some of the most beautiful places you will ever find. If you ever see the Secret Theatre in its finished form, you will understand.

What happens in theatres is equally beautiful, and this is the second meaning of the word. Theatre is performance, it is acting out a story with an audience in front of you. Each actor (male performer) or actress (female performer) plays the part of a character and brings them to life. Again, this does no justice to what performance is, so let me simply say that the atmosphere created by it, and the feeling that both the actors and the audience get, is incredible.

Well, I think that will do for now. I must return to help with preparations for the Secret Theatre! I hope that this has been interesting for you so far, and in future entries I promise that I will show you just how special theatre is.

With love,
Emily

CHAPTER 6

Unwrapping the Mystery

As Becky walked up through the graveyard she saw the vicar ahead of her, greeting everyone entering the church for the council meeting. She had always liked visiting the church, with its funny crooked spire and perfectly planted grounds, but right now all she wanted was to be in her room reading more of Emily's diary.

'Stand up straight, Becky,' said her mum for the tenth time. 'Best behaviour when we get in.'

When they entered the meeting room, Becky and her mum took the two remaining seats at the end of the large oak table that filled most of the room. The vicar was sitting opposite them at the head of the table, with the other seven members of the council spread around it. The setting sun coming in through the stained glass window gave the room a warm feeling.

'Right, I call this meeting of July the fifth to order,' said the vicar, who was wearing a bright red jumper that stood out against the dark wall behind him.

He started by announcing changes in Church service times for the next week, and was followed by the woolly-haired Mrs Didsbury, who needed money to repair her knitting stall in the market; then Albert Gailsborough, the oldest and wrinkliest of Thistlewick's fishermen, droned on about the fishing festival he had attended the previous week. Soon any interest that Becky might have had in the meeting had been sucked away.

It's all so boring, she thought, *compared to what's happening in my life.*

Emily had been right in her diary – the theatre was the most beautiful room Becky had ever been in, and she was desperate to find out more about it. In her mind she saw the wonderful reds and golds, the smiling masks, the huge curtain on the platform…

'Barbara, how can we help you?'

Becky's attention was jerked back to the meeting by the vicar's words.

Her mum placed the parcel on the table.

'I have this parcel,' she began, 'addressed to Emily Wilson at Midsummer House—'

'Throw it away!' Albert cut her off.

Becky turned to face him – that was the quickest she'd seen him react to anything.

'Why do you say that, Albert?' asked the vicar calmly.

'It's addressed to *her*. Get rid of it!'

Becky's mouth almost fell open – how could Albert talk about Emily like that?

'It's harmless, Albie, just a piece of post,' said Ted Castle.

Albert frowned at his fellow fisherman. 'You don't know that. It could just as well be dang'rous!'

'Well, even if it is, we need to establish the facts,' said the vicar. 'Barbara, did you try to deliver the parcel?'

'Against my wishes, Becky tried to deliver it, but as we could all have guessed, there was no response when she knocked on the door.'

Becky's mum glared briefly at her, as if to reinforce that it had been wrong of her to go in the first place. And Becky couldn't fail to see the grave look on Albert's face, even through all his wrinkles. Why was he so against Emily?

'Is the parcel a new one?' asked the vicar.

'Yes, it's postmarked the twenty-third of last month and arrived today.'

'That is most int'restin',' said Ted. 'Whoever sent it is over fifty years too late if they were hopin' to reach Emily Wilson.'

'And a good job too,' said Albert.

Becky put her hand up.

'Becky, do you have a question?' asked the vicar.

'Yes,' she replied. 'How come Midsummer House is so rundown? And what happened to Emily Wilson?'

She looked around the council members. Her question was met with silence, and everyone looked at each other, as if waiting for someone else to answer. The vicar coughed and Mrs Didsbury played with her hair nervously.

It was Albert who spoke at last. 'That's not somethin' young people should know about.'

'Why not?' Becky asked. But this question got no further than a warning stare from her mum. Becky slouched down in her seat and frowned.

'Right,' said the vicar. 'Let's vote on what to do with the parcel. Please raise your hand to indicate your preferred decision. All those in favour of throwing it away…'

Albert put his hand up immediately. He glared around the table and eventually Mrs Didsbury raised her hand too.

'All those in favour of opening it to find out what's inside…'

The rest of the council, and Becky, raised their hands. If they opened the parcel, she thought, its contents might tell her something else about Emily, or the Secret Theatre.

'Very well, we have a clear decision. Barbara, if you'd like to hand me the parcel.'

Becky followed the parcel as her mum passed it down the table. She leaned forwards and noticed all the council members, except Albert, do the same. The vicar peeled away the tape and neatly unwrapped the outer paper.

Inside was another parcel, and sitting on top of it was a letter.

'*Dear Miss Wilson,*' the vicar read. '*Please find enclosed a parcel addressed to yourself. According to its postmark it is coming to you considerably late. I offer my sincere apologies for this – I have only just discovered it while sorting through boxes – but I hope that it finds you in the best of health. Yours sincerely, John Charlton, head of the Postal Service on the mainland.*'

'Well, this really is too late for Emily,' said Ted.

The vicar placed the second parcel on the table. 'The postmark says it was sent on the seventh of August nineteen fifty-two, from the Drapery Furnishing Company. Shall we open it?'

Albert shook his head, but it was clear that the rest of the council wanted to see what was inside.

As the vicar started to unwrap the second parcel, Becky saw that it was a lot older – the paper was thin and flakey and the tape the vicar peeled off came away with ease. A small bundle of material was revealed, which the vicar unravelled. It fell down in a long strip.

Becky stared at it.

'There's a note,' said the vicar. '*Here is the sample material – royal red as requested. We hope you like what we have sent you enough to consider placing an order with Drapery Furnishing.*'

'Maybe she was planning to buy new curtains,' suggested Mrs Didsbury.

'It was meant for the Secret Theatre,' Becky said. The material was the same colour she had seen covering the whole theatre.

'What was that, girl?' asked Albert.

'That material was for the Secret Theatre.'

The council members stared at each other; Ted's eyes widened.

'That's enough, Becky,' her mum said.

'Theatre?!' Albert shouted.

Becky jumped in her seat – she had never heard Albert shout before.

'Theatre!' he repeated. 'First you come here talkin' of Emily Wilson and now theatre!' He stood up and stared straight at her. 'There is no theatre on Thistlewick. I do not know where you got the idea from or how you know about theatre, but it stops now! You must not go near Midsummer House again. That place is dang'rous!'

CHAPTER 7

The Thistlewick Thespians

Becky was confused. In her diary, Emily had said she was building the theatre as a fight against 'them'. Was Albert one of 'them' then? He clearly hadn't liked Emily or theatre, or he wouldn't have reacted so angrily when Becky had mentioned them. But she couldn't understand *why* he was so against them.

Emily had also mentioned 'we' – that she would explain who 'we' were in future entries. She must have meant the people who fought with her and built the theatre. But why was there no fight now? Why was Midsummer House abandoned?

There's only one way to answer these questions.

She got off her bed and unlocked her secret drawer, where she usually kept people's birthday presents along with her hidden stash of sweets. Out of the drawer she took the red-covered diary.

Opening it to the second entry, she let Emily's words fill her mind.

July 29th 1952

Everything at the Secret Theatre is going well. We've marked out where all the different parts will be placed, and in a few days I should receive diagrams for the theatre, so I'll tell you all about our plans then.

It's going to take a long time to get all the building materials here. Most of them will have to be brought in in secret, so that 'they' don't catch us.

There I go mentioning 'them' again. I said in the last entry I would explain who 'they' are. But I also promised that I would explain who 'we' are, and I think that we are far more worthy of my ink, so it is only right that I start here.

We are a group of people who are fighting to save theatre on Thistlewick Island. There are fifteen of us, of all ages and sizes. (I'm one of the smallest!) Some of us are fishermen, others are farm workers; there's young Cyril who is only ten and old Bernie who is nearly eighty. Together we are the Thistlewick Thespians!

Thespian simply means an actor or actress, and the word is a tribute to the first actor ever known, a Greek man called Thespis, who lived all the way back in the sixth century. (I hope you find this fact interesting – you'll find a lot of trivia about theatre in this diary. I can't help but love it!)

The Thistlewick Thespians had a wonderful life together. We performed pieces of theatre around Thistlewick, to the workers at the White Wing Pub on Friday nights and to the congregation at the Church every Sunday. It always brings a smile to my face thinking of the joy we shared with everyone, as well as the amazing feeling of performing together. We didn't need one building to perform in, for the whole of Thistlewick was our theatre. But then 'they' came and it all changed.

Becky heard footsteps thundering up the stairs.

She looked up from the diary and nearly fell off her bed when she saw the tall, dark-haired figure standing in the doorway. She quickly hid the diary under her pillow.

'Haven't you heard of a thing called knocking before you come into someone's room?' she said to her brother.

'Well, you were so engrossed in that book that you obviously didn't hear me. I knocked so loudly that the whole island opened their doors to see who was there, everyone except you,' smirked William.

'Yeah, very funny.'

'So, why is my little sister hiding things from me?'

'I'm not hiding anything,' Becky said.

'Of course not. I obviously imagined you shoving that book under your pillow the second you saw me.'

He moved further into the room. Becky sat up on the pillow – she didn't want her brother, of all people, to know about the diary. Not yet.

'Will, you're filthy. You're making my room dirty.'

Her brother was covered in mud, and he'd obviously just returned from working on Ben and Harriet's tree house.

'Not as dirty as that lie you just told me. You look really guilty now.'

Becky gave him her most fearsome glare.

'Fine, you keep your secrets, I'm going for a bath.' He started to leave the room, but when he got to the door he turned around again. 'I bet that book's something to do with Midsummer House though.'

Becky's eyes widened.

'Yeah, Mum told me all about your little adventure. I mean, honestly, while I'm out doing a hard day's labour, you're off trying to break into houses. I bet you haven't told Mum about that book, have you?'

'You won't tell her, will you?'

William stared at her very seriously. Then his expression changed into a wide grin. ''Course not!'

And with that he was gone, slamming the door behind him.

Becky breathed a sigh of relief and removed the diary from under the pillow, desperate to find out who 'they' were.

'They' are known as the 'Renegade Group', led by an evil man called Simon Renegade. We are forced to call him Lord Renegade. He thinks he is noble, like Lord Thistlewick, who created our island, but Renegade is no Lord. He took our island by force eight months ago. In that time, he has turned it into a sort of prison, where we have to work all day on the farms. He has ripped away every aspect of our lives that might give us enjoyment, and banned the pub, the market, music and theatre.

Most of the islanders are too scared of the Renegade Group to do anything. But banning theatre – that is a crime I cannot stand.

That is why we, the Thistlewick Thespians, are fighting back.

Becky closed the diary slowly.

The Renegade Group had banned theatre on Thistlewick, and they had fought against Emily Wilson.

That means, Becky thought gravely, *that Albert Gailsborough must be a member of the Renegade Group.*

CHAPTER 8
Production

Becky walked out of her house and into the empty Market Square at seven o'clock the next morning. It was her mum's only day for a lie-in, and she was still safely in bed.

Becky set off along the path to Midsummer House. She'd thought about asking Jimmy along, but his mum always woke up early and would have been suspicious about where they were going.

He'd be scared of coming again anyway, she thought as she walked out of the square.

In no time at all she had reached the rusty gate leading to Midsummer House. It was a lot easier now she knew where she was going. As she walked up the garden path she saw a small bird – a goldfinch – twittering away on the arm of the wheelbarrow full of stinging nettles. Its bright yellow breast stood out brilliantly against the untamed garden.

'Albert obviously hasn't shouted at you not to come here,' she said to it.

She still couldn't believe that he had been a member of the Renegade Group. From what Emily had said, they sounded really horrible, and she had never thought of Albert as being horrible. But what other reason would he have for his views?

I'll have to try and find out more about the Renegade Group, she told herself.

***

A few minutes later, Becky found her excitement level rising and her heart beating faster as she pulled at the book with the title *Theatre: A Beginner's Guide*. The bookcase shot to one side, Becky turned the golden masked doorknob and walked into the Secret Theatre.

She had thought about this moment all through the night, and still wasn't prepared for the effect the room had on her for the second time. It was such a beautiful, powerful place.

Becky took the diary out of her bag, unwrapped it from the spare jumper she'd used to protect it and opened it to the third entry, dated 1st August 1952.

Emily had received the plans and, as promised, took Becky through all the different parts that would make up the theatre.

She had copied the diagram of the planned theatre into the diary, and Becky used this as a sort of map.

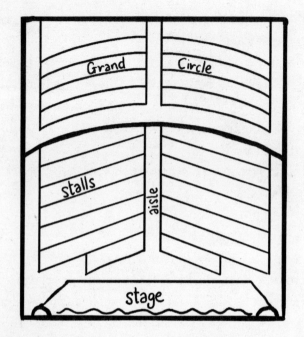

First she walked up onto the platform, or, as Emily called it, 'the stage, where the performance is acted out'.

Then Becky slowly moved around the rest of the theatre and ten minutes later, she knew exactly what each part was called.

It was strange reading about the plans for the theatre from before it was built, while standing in it over fifty years later; but at the same time there was something about reading the diary in the very place it described that made it even more special, and made Becky feel much closer to Emily Wilson.

The entry also listed the names of all the Thistlewick Thespians, and talked about a new production they were going to put on.

We were about to start working on it before 'they' came, and I won't let 'them' stop us from doing it now! It is our most ambitious production yet. Once we have finished building the Secret Theatre, we will have a much better space in which to bring the production to life. It is called 'The Magic Paintbrush'.

Becky wondered if the Thespians ever had managed to perform 'The Magic Paintbrush' in front of an audience. She looked up at the stage and imagined people standing on it holding paint brushes in the air, and wished that she could put her own production on at the Secret Theatre, even though she didn't quite know what that meant.

***

As the bookcase closed behind her and she began to move towards the library door, Becky spotted the photos on the mantelpiece. She remembered the one of the big group of people in funny costumes.

They must be the Thistlewick Thespians.

She walked over and picked up the photo. When she had first looked at it, she'd wondered why all the Thespians were wearing silly outfits.

It must be from when they were putting on a production.

She opened the diary to the

page that listed the Thespians to see if she could identify any of them in the photo. There was Emily, of course, who Becky was now sure was the lovely woman in the other photo on the mantelpiece, and the young boy must be Cyril Silverdale…

'only ten, the youngest of us all, but also the most talented and the one with the biggest smile.'

Cyril was only ten when they'd started *The Magic Paintbrush* – Becky was older than that now. Maybe she really would be able to put on her own production…

Looking back at the photo, she wondered how a sailor boy fitted into the same story as a group of medieval knights. One of the knights looked quite like Ted Castle, the fisherman, and had the same bushy eyebrows. On the list, Becky found the name Philip Castle…

'not only a great actor, he is also the guiding force in building the theatre. He takes the great risk of gathering all our building materials and bringing them to us at night, under the nose of the Renegade Group. We couldn't do it without him.'

That must be have been Ted's dad, and therefore Jack's granddad.

She couldn't put any of the other names to faces, but the photo clearly showed how close and happy the Thistlewick Thespians were. The image of people standing on stage holding paintbrushes came into her mind again, but this time they were the Thespians from the photo. She glanced back at the diary and read the line Emily had written under the list of names.

'Together, we are the Thistlewick Thespians. Without any of these people the theatre simply wouldn't work, and I wouldn't be able to turn my dreams into reality.'

Suddenly Becky realised what Emily meant – you couldn't work a theatre or put on a production all by yourself. If Becky wanted to put on her own production, she would have to get other people involved. She had to tell someone else about the Secret Theatre.

But who?

She'd already told Jimmy, but they needed more than just the two of them. Who else would believe her?

Ben and Harriet!

After all, on their adventure the previous year, the twins had encountered things that no one thought existed. If anyone would believe Becky, it was Ben and Harriet.

She looked at her watch. It was half past eight – if she hurried back now, by the time she got to their house, they should just be awake. Becky placed the photo back on the mantelpiece, gathered up her belongings and ran out through the library door.

CHAPTER 9
A Secret Shared

Becky knocked on Jimmy's front door. She'd decided it would be good to have him there to back her story up when she saw Harriet and Ben.

The door opened quickly and Jimmy appeared.

'I saw you coming,' he said, then he called back into the house, 'Mum, I'm just going out with Becky.'

'Where are you going?' Becky thought Jimmy's mum's voice sounded slightly sterner than usual.

Jimmy looked to Becky.

'Just to Harriet and Ben's house,' she said.

'I don't want you to go anywhere else, ok? Be back by lunchtime, Jimmy.'

Jimmy stepped out through the door.

They walked through the Market Square in silence. Becky knew something was wrong with her friend.

'You haven't told anyone about Midsummer House have you, Jimmy?' she eventually asked as they walked along a coastal path.

Jimmy stared ahead. 'No,' he said quietly. 'But your mum told my mum about it. Why did you have to say I was with you? My mum nearly went mad and I had to tell her I didn't go in. I don't like lying to her.'

'So that's why she sounded a bit cross. Sorry... Anyway, I can't wait for you to see the theatre.'

'Your mum told my mum it was "ridiculous nonsense".'

'The theatre isn't ridiculous nonsense! It's real, Jimmy, and it's so amazing! You do believe me, don't you?'

'Er... of course.'

'Good, then let's hope the twins do too.'

***

Becky settled herself into the plump armchair in the Davies's living room.

'So what do you want to tell us about, Becky?' asked Harriet.

Before Becky had had a chance to reply, the front doorbell rang.

'I'll just get that,' said Ben.

A few seconds later he returned, and someone else was with him.

'Hello, sis,' said William. 'I just came round to finish off the tree house. Why are you here?'

'Becky's got something to tell us. Is it ok if Will knows your secret as well?' Ben asked her.

'You promise you won't tell Mum?' Becky asked.

'Yep, promise,' said William.

She looked long and hard at her brother, trying to figure out if he was telling the truth.

'You'll find out soon anyway,' she sighed.

So Becky began her story, as Harriet, Ben, Jimmy and William sat around her listening closely.

'Yesterday I picked up a parcel addressed to Midsummer House, which I'd never heard of, so I went to find it…'

She explained all about what had happened, right up to her discovery of the theatre. When she said the word 'theatre', the others looked puzzled.

'Theatre? Where have I heard that word before?' asked Harriet.

'There's a place called a theatre on the mainland,' said Ben. 'I always wondered what it was, but I was never allowed in.'

'Me neither,' Becky said. 'But there's definitely one on Thistlewick, and I've found it.'

She went on to tell them about Emily's diary and the fight between the Thistlewick Thespians and the Renegade Group, and about Albert Gailsborough being part of it.

'Wow, that's incredible, Becky!' exclaimed Harriet.

'Some secret you were hiding,' said William.

'I can't wait to see the theatre!' said Ben, his eyes eager.

'So you believe me, then?' Becky asked. 'None of the adults do.'

'Becky, we specialise in finding things no one thought existed. Of course we believe you,' said Harriet.

'Thank you.' Becky felt her face light up, and she grinned a bigger grin than she had done all year.

'I wonder why none of the adults believe the theatre is there, though?' said William.

'I don't know, but it's got something to do with Albert and the Renegade Group.'

'Can we go and see it now?' asked Ben.

***

As Becky placed her hand on *Theatre: A Beginner's Guide*, she noticed another book beside it, which had a familiar name. *The Magic Paintbrush.*

The play the Thespians performed!

She pulled it out and carried it with her as the bookcase slid out of the way and she walked through into the Secret Theatre, followed by the others.

As the light flicked on, she heard a gasp behind her. She turned around and watched her friends' first reactions to the theatre. Ben's eyes widened; Jimmy, who had originally been unsure about entering, stared in awe around the place; Harriet smiled at the beauty of it and William's mouth fell open.

Becky hoped that when she'd first seen the theatre her reaction hadn't been like her brother's, but more like Harriet's.

'What happens… in a theatre?' asked Jimmy, his voice full of wonder.

'People called actors perform stories in front of an audience.' Becky said.

They moved forwards and Becky climbed up onto the stage.

'I wonder why we've never learnt about theatre at school,' said William.

'Well, if theatre was banned on Thistlewick years ago, Mr Harris probably isn't allowed to teach us about it,' said Harriet.

'Wouldn't it be cool to do something in here though,' said Ben.

'Then why don't we?' Becky said. 'It's called "putting on a production". Emily and the Thespians were doing one called *The Magic Paintbrush* when the Renegade Group came. And look what I've just found.'

As she showed them the book, she noticed that on the cover was written 'by Emily Wilson'.

'Wow! I didn't realise Emily wrote it! She was obviously a really talented person. We should definitely put on *The Magic Paintbrush*!'

'That's a great idea, Becky,' said Harriet.

'How many of us do we need to put on a production?' asked William. 'Surely more than five?'

'There were fifteen Thistlewick Thespians,' Becky said. 'So we do need more people, I think.'

'Will, why don't we ask around tomorrow?' said Ben. 'I'm sure we can get most of our friends to come along.'

'Yeah, I'm up for that.'

'We also need to find out more about the Renegade Group and why they banned theatre,' Becky said. 'I'm stuck serving in the post office tomorrow, though.'

'That's perfect, Becky, you can ask all the customers about it. I'll go along and talk to the vicar. He probably has lots of information in his Book of Records,' said Harriet.

'And I'll have a look for books about the Renegade Group in the library,' said Jimmy.

'We'll meet back here in two days' time, then.' Becky said.

CHAPTER 10

Mrs Didsbury

'Could I have a five penny stamp, please?' asked little Bertie Granger.

'Here you go, Bertie,' Becky said, handing him the small green stamp. 'Who's your letter for?'

'It's a card for my granddaddy's birthday. Made it myself!'

'That's nice. Put it in the post box when you've stuck the stamp on. Have a good day.'

Have a good day. She'd been saying that to lots of people throughout the morning, but none of them had looked old enough to know anything about the Renegade Group.

She walked out of the main post office and into the small side kitchen to get a drink. When she returned, Ted Castle was standing in front of the counter.

Maybe he's old enough.

'Hello, Becky. I've got to return this fishin' gear to the mainland and I'm not goin' over there for a week or two. How much would it cost to post all fifteen kilograms of it?'

She found the sheet that told her and scanned down the different weights. 'Twelve pounds, Mr Castle.'

'Becky, you should know by now, you can call me Ted. I'll go for that postage, then.'

'Ted?' Becky said as she sorted out his order. 'Why did the Renegade Group come to Thistlewick?'

She looked up. Ted's bushy eyebrows had gathered in a deep frown.

'Well I don't know how you heard of them, but you best not let Albie catch you talkin' like that, not after the council meetin' you came to.'

'Oh. Why not?'

'Sorry, Becky, I can't say any more on the matter.'

Half an hour later, Mr Potts, the farmer, came in. He was sending off an order for more checkered shirts to add to his collection. Becky asked him the same question and his response was similar to Ted's. But when Sergeant Radley, with his moustache upturned in its own smile, walked through the door, Becky felt sure that he would tell her something.

'I don't have instruction to discuss that sort of thing. You would be wise not to mention it to anyone again.' The sergeant's moustache twitched and he walked out without even taking the stamps that he'd bought.

Why will no one tell me anything?

If the Renegade Group had come sixty years ago and taken over Thistlewick, that was a pretty big part of the island's history. So how was it that Becky knew nothing about it?

Maybe people are too scared to talk about it – they're probably too frightened of Albert to say anything.

Every time she thought about it, it always came down to Albert Gailsborough – he was the person behind a lot of this, she was sure.

The next person to enter the post office was Mrs Didsbury. As she browsed around the stationery shelf, Becky decided to try a different question on her.

'Mrs Didsbury?'

'Yes, my dear.'

'Is Albert still part of the Renegade Group?'

The elderly woman almost staggered back into the shelf. 'Albert... a part of... of... the Renegade Group? How could you think such a thing? The Renegade Group were evil, evil people, Becky.' She leaned against the shelf to support herself. 'They treated my poor husband, Arthur, so badly.'

'How, Mrs Didsbury?'

'He was a farm labourer. When Renegade came with his followers, they forced us all to work day and night. We weren't allowed to enjoy ourselves, just work. And that's what caused my Arthur to break his leg – he was so tired from all the working that one day he just fell, from the top of a haystack. They had no sympathy for him.'

'I'm sorry, Mrs Didsbury.' Becky really was – it sounded awful. But she also sensed that she could get more information out of the old lady. 'Why did the Renegade Group come to Thistlewick?'

Mrs Didsbury took in a deep breath. 'It was over a fight between the Renegade family and the Thistlewick family. They both had a lot of power in the farming world, but unlike Lord Thistlewick, the Renegades had gained power by being ruthless and treating their farms like prisons. Lord Thistlewick campaigned against their treatment of their workers, and because of this the Renegades had always threatened to capture the island Thistlewick had created – our island. It was in nineteen fifty-two that Simon Renegade finally did.'

'And they banned all the entertainment on Thistlewick?'

'Yes.'

'Including theatre?'

'Becky, you mustn't mention that word.' Suddenly Mrs Didsbury's voice became quite sharp. 'It's still banned on our island, and for good reason.'

'But I don't understand. Albert...'

'Albert was not a member of the Renegade Group, you must never let that thought cross your mind again. Now, I've said too much.' Her voice started to soften to its usual tone again. 'You must forgive me, I get very emotional when I think back to those times. I... I must get back to my stall.'

She returned a pencil to the shelf and left.

CHAPTER 11
Auditions

'Well, Becky, you found out more than I did,' said Harriet. 'The vicar wouldn't let me look in the Book of Records for the Renegade Group. He said it should only be used to find information that's good for the island.'

'The only thing I found in the library was a small mention in this book.' Jimmy handed Becky *Thistlewick: the Timeline*. 'It says they came on the twelfth of January nineteen fifty-two and left on the third of September the same year.'

'They weren't here that long, then,' said Harriet.

'No, but they left someone behind,' Becky said.

'I thought Mrs Didsbury said Albert wasn't a member of the Renegade Group?'

'I don't think she's telling the truth. The only reason he can be so against theatre is if he was part of that group.'

'Can you hurry up and tell us what we're here for?' came Jack's voice.

Becky turned around to face the collection of children sitting in the stalls below her.

Two of her friends, at least, had been successful in their task. Ben and William had managed to convince nine more children to come along, which meant there were now fourteen of them in the Secret Theatre – only one less than there were in the original Thistlewick Thespians.

'We're here,' she said from the stage, 'to continue the fight of the Thistlewick Thespians. Many years ago theatre was banned on Thistlewick, but the Thespians tried to fight back. We're going to continue their fight, by putting on a production.'

'So what's the first step, Becky?' asked Harriet.

'I was reading Emily's diary last night, and it's something called auditions, where we decide who will be acting as each character in *The Magic Paintbrush*.'

She opened the book of *The Magic Paintbrush* to the first page, where there was a list of all the characters.

'The main character is a boy called Andrew, who through the story turns into a really good painter,' Becky said. 'I think Jimmy should be Andrew, because he can paint really well. Plus he's the same age as Andrew.'

Cast List

Andrew
Andrew's mother
Duchess Viroqua
Lord Thickwistle
Lady Thickwistle
Forest Tribe
Philip the Painter
The Queen
Maids and Servants

She looked down to Jimmy, who was sitting quietly to one side of the stage.

'Jimmy, do you want to be the main character?' asked Harriet.

'Yeah, ok.'

'Let's take a vote, then. Who thinks Jimmy should play Andrew?' Becky asked.

Most of the children put their hands up.

And so it continued. Other characters were chosen, until they got to the character Becky really wanted to play.

'The Queen. Andrew paints her, and she threatens to behead him if she doesn't like his painting. Hands up if you want to play the Queen.'

Becky put her own hand up, and so did two other girls – Catherine Wheeler and Isabel Starr.

'So, who's it going to be?' asked Harriet.

'Catherine, what do you think the Queen should be like?' asked Ben.

'A bit like a fairy, maybe,' said Catherine, in a very girly voice.

'And Issie, what about you?'

'I dunno. Normal, I guess,' Isabel replied in a bored tone.

'What about you, Becky?'

'I think she should be really scary and evil.'

'Show us,' said Jack.

Becky thought for a minute, and tried to imagine herself having an argument with her mum.

'How dare you speak to me like that!' she shouted.

To her delight, she saw Jack's eyes widen. 'That's actually quite scary,' he said.

'So who should it be?' said Harriet.

'Even though she's my sister, I think it should be Becky,' said William. 'If this Queen is supposed to threaten Andrew with being beheaded, then she has to be pretty evil, like Becky was there.'

Becky grinned at her brother. There was a murmur of agreement around the other children.

'So, all those who think Becky should be the Queen,' said Ben.

Eight hands went up.

'Yes!' Becky exclaimed.

***

'What's next?' Ben asked, once the 'auditions', as Emily called them, had finished.

'I'm not sure,' Becky said.

She realised then that even though she had been reading Emily's diary and knew what everything in the theatre was called, she didn't actually know *how* to put on a production.

'I only got as far as reading about auditions.'

'Can you read the next bit then?' asked Jack.

'I'm not really a fast reader,' Becky admitted. 'It'll take me quite a long time.'

'I'll have a read,' said Isabel. 'I'm pretty fast. Give me the diary, Becky.'

'No,' Becky said. There was no way she was going to let it out of her sight, especially for Isabel Starr.

'What we really need,' announced William, 'is to find

someone to help us who knows a lot about theatre. It's going to be pretty tricky learning it all from a book.'

'But if theatre's banned, there won't be anyone on the island who knows about it,' said Ben.

'Hang on!' A thought had suddenly struck Becky.

She jumped down from the stage and ran past the others, out into the library. From the mantelpiece she grabbed the photo of the Thistlewick Thespians and charged back into the theatre.

'Look!' she called, stopping abruptly at the front. Everyone gathered around as she showed them the photo. 'These are the Thistlewick Thespians. I wonder if any of them are still alive.'

'They all look pretty old to me,' said Ben.

'Wait a minute,' said Jack. 'That's my granddad!'

'He was one of the Thistlewick Thespians,' Becky said.

'I never knew that. Wait till I tell Dad!'

'You can't tell your dad about any of this,' said William. 'He's Albert's best friend, isn't he?'

'Oh… yeah,' said Jack, a bit disappointed.

'I think they'll all be dead now, Becky,' said Ben.

'Apart from…' Becky began. She was staring at the young boy in the sailor's outfit. 'Cyril Silverdale! He was only ten when Emily wrote the diary.'

'That means he'd be in his sixties now. How can we find out if he's still alive?' asked Harriet.

'We need to go to the post office,' Becky said.

CHAPTER 12

The Last Thistlewick Thespian

'Locked in the cupboard in the sorting room is a book with the name of everyone who's lived on Thistlewick for the past two hundred years,' Becky explained to Jimmy, Ben, Harriet and William, who had come back with her to the post office.

They stared in through the window, watching Becky's mum serving Sergeant Radley.

'Mum's the only one who's meant to look in it, so someone needs to distract her while I go around to get it.'

She looked at Jimmy.

'You know I'm useless at that sort of thing,' he said.

'I'll do it,' said Ben. 'I'll say I'm doing a summer project about stamps or something.'

William frowned at him. 'The great adventurer, Ben Davies, doing a project about stamps?'

Ben shrugged. 'Stops me getting into trouble.'

'The only problem now is finding the key to unlock the cupboard,' Becky said.

'It's on the top shelf in the sorting room,' said William. 'I saw Mum put it up there a while ago. You'll have to use a stool to reach it.'

'Right, so if you go in now, Ben, I'll go round the back way into the sorting room. You'll need to keep Mum in the main post office for about five minutes.'

***

As Becky slipped through the back door into the sorting room, she heard her mum speaking.

'Hello, Ben. You haven't seen Becky, have you?'

Becky froze.

'No, Mrs Evans.'

'Honestly, I don't know where she's got to. She's in my bad books as it is, and I've just had Sergeant Radley in here complaining that she's been saying things she shouldn't. She hasn't said anything to you, has she?'

'No, Mrs Evans.' Ben sounded quite convincing, Becky thought.

'Anyway, how can I help you, Ben?'

Becky moved as quietly as she could past the piles of post over to the stool in the corner. She picked it up and placed it at the centre of the shelving, which stretched from floor to ceiling on the left hand wall.

As she stepped onto it she caught a few words of Ben's conversation about stamps.

'…and what's the largest stamp in the world?'

'Let me see. It's the…'

'Penny farthing,' Becky mouthed as her mum said it. She couldn't quite reach the top shelf with her hand and stretched up on tiptoes. She felt the stool start to wobble beneath her, and as she tried to regain her balance it rocked from side to side, making two loud thuds on the hard floor.

'What was that?' she heard her mum ask.

'Mrs Evans, how many stamps are bought from your post office each year?' Ben said quickly, and it seemed to distract her.

Becky carefully stretched up again and felt along the top shelf with her hand. Eventually she found metal and lifted down the old silver key.

She moved over to the cupboard. This was the riskiest part, as it was right next to the door into the main post office. She unlocked it.

'So, what does a British stamp look like?' Ben was asking. 'Does it have a picture of their Queen on it?'

'Oh, I think I actually received a parcel from Britain today. I'll just get it from the back.'

Becky's stomach turned as she heard her mum's footsteps coming towards the door.

'No, actually, it's ok, Mrs Evans,' said Ben, who obviously realised what was happening.

'It's no trouble, Ben, it's just on the side in here.'

Becky panicked as the door started to open. She looked to the cupboard she had just opened and quickly dived inside, closing the door as she heard her mum come into the room.

Trying not to breathe, she waited in the darkness as her mum shuffled about, humming as she tried to find the parcel from Britain. Becky hoped she wouldn't notice that the stool had moved.

What felt like many minutes later, Becky heard her mum's retreating footsteps. She slowly opened the cupboard door and breathed a sigh of relief as light hit her. She searched around the cupboard and soon found the book she was looking for.

Sitting down on the floor, she opened it up. It was organised by year of birth.

If Cyril was ten in nineteen fifty-two, that means he would have been born in… nineteen forty-two.

She quickly flicked through the pages and found the right year. Scanning down the list she came to the name. Cyril Silverdale.

Please say he's still alive.

She looked along the entry. *Born 13th August. Died…* there was nothing in the 'died' column – he was still alive! Under the address column, she saw that he had been living at the White Wing Pub and Hotel for the last ten years.

'Thank you for all your help, Mrs Evans,' said Ben.

It was time for Becky to leave. She shut the book.

'My pleasure, Ben. It's good that someone is taking an interest in the postal service. If you see Becky on your travels, tell her I want to see her.'

'Will do.'

Becky locked the cupboard and threw the key back up onto the top shelf, before running out through the back door again.

***

She walked up to the others, who were waiting on a bench in the Market Square.

'Thanks, Ben. You did really well,' she said.

'We were nearly in trouble there, though,' he said. 'How did you hide when your mum went into the back room?'

Becky told him about hiding in the cupboard.

'Anyway, Cyril's alive,' she said. 'And he lives at the White Wing!'

'Excellent, so are you going to go and ask him if he'll help with our production?' asked Harriet.

'Yep, and hopefully he'll be able to tell me more about why the Renegade Group banned theatre as well.'

'Right, well we've got a tree house to finish building,' said Ben. 'So come and find us tomorrow, Becky. We'll want to know how it goes.'

He waved goodbye as he left with Harriet and William.

'Come on, Jimmy,' Becky said, 'let's go and see Cyril.'

CHAPTER 13

Cyril

The White Wing Pub and Hotel was a quaint sort of place now, but had once been the home of Lord Thistlewick himself, so had very grand features. Becky had learnt about it at school. The bar area was lit by a big chandelier, similar to the one in the Secret Theatre, and had a very large fireplace, which crackled cheerfully on cold winter nights. The room was packed with dark wooden tables and very comfortable chairs. A lot of Thistlewickians liked to come here to unwind after a hard day's work.

As Becky and Jimmy entered, though, it was quite quiet – most of the islanders were still working. There were only a couple of elderly residents, staring out of the windows at the magnificent sea view, and the landlady, Pat Galway, who was filling in a crossword behind the bar.

'The Thistlewick Thespians used to perform here every Friday night,' Becky explained to Jimmy. 'Before the Renegade Group came.'

She looked around. There would have been lots of people sitting in the cosy chairs, sipping drinks and enjoying the performances. She couldn't quite picture where in the pub the Thespians would have performed, though – perhaps in front of a roaring fire, with Emily standing there in her long, flowing dress.

'That would have been impressive,' Becky said under her breath.

But then she remembered she didn't know what a performance involved.

That's what I'm here to find out.

'What can I do for you, children?' Pat Galway asked from the bar.

'We'd like to see Cyril Silverdale, please,' Becky said.

'Oh, right. Well you can, I s'pose,' said Pat, looking slightly surprised. 'But he don't receive many visitors and he's havin' a bad day today. What d'you want to see him for?'

The landlady's question seemed more out of curiosity than suspicion.

Becky thought she'd use the same excuse Ben used at the post office. 'It's for a school summer project. We want to interview him.'

'Oh aye, what about?'

Becky turned to Jimmy and gave him an 'it's your turn' look.

'We have to choose an elderly Thistlewickian to ask what they most enjoy about living on the island and what else they would benefit from. We chose Mr Silverdale,' he said quickly, as if reciting something that their teacher, Mr Harris, had told them.

Becky was impressed – for someone who didn't like lying, Jimmy was very good at it. She nodded at the landlady to confirm what he'd said.

'Well, I'll tell you what Cyril would benefit from – a good cheerin' up. He's a grumpy old so-and-so a lot of the time, and I'll warn you that he don't usually take kindly to visitors. But maybe you two'll be able to put a smile on his face.'

'Which room is he in?' Becky asked.

'Cyril's on the second floor, room seventy-three.'

***

They walked along the brightly lit corridor until they came to the white painted door of room seventy-three. Becky knocked, then knocked again, and when there was no answer she opened the door slowly.

The room in front of her was dark in contrast to the brightness of the hallway. There were no lights on in it and the curtains were drawn.

It took her a while to spot the man sitting in the chair. As she looked at him, Becky thought he seemed like a deflated balloon – it was as if the life had seeped out of him very slowly, and he had been reduced to a shrivelled heap, hunched in a chair in the dark corner of a small room.

The room itself had no personality. It was old like the man, but in an untouched way, as if it hadn't been used for years; yet Becky imagined that he had lived in it for all that time. There was a single bed next to his chair, and a wardrobe at the end of that. Next to Becky was a sink with a small mirror over it; she couldn't see any photos on the walls. There was only one object that had any colour to it – a small red box sitting next to the man's chair.

As she stood in the doorway he didn't seem to notice her. Instead he was staring at the drawn curtains, which covered what would have been a lovely view out to sea.

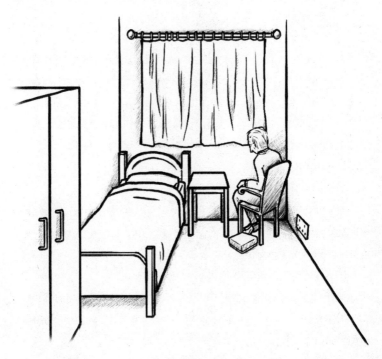

Hello Cyril, she thought, but she couldn't quite bring herself to say it.

Then the old man turned slowly to face her.

'What do you want?' said Cyril, in a voice that had no expression.

His eyes were sad and drawn into his face, as if they hadn't seen happiness for a long time, and had given up looking for it. But Becky sensed that he *had* once been happy, that he had been full of life… a long time ago.

'Ms Galway said we could come up to see you,' she said.

Becky hesitated, but moved into the room slightly, and felt Jimmy pressing in behind her.

'Well, what is it?'

He had changed so much from the grinning boy wearing the sailor's outfit in the photo at Midsummer House that Becky wasn't actually certain this *was* Cyril. Perhaps she'd entered the wrong room, and Cyril was next door reciting a play he'd just written, waiting for the chance to perform it.

I'd better check.

'Cyril?' she asked.

'Yes.'

So it definitely was Cyril, the youngest member of the Thistlewick Thespians. But what had turned him into such a sad old man?

'My name is Becky, and this is Jimmy.'

Jimmy gave him a small smile.

'You were… no, you *are* a Thistlewick Thespian, aren't you?' she said.

Cyril said nothing, but his face changed – his lips pursed together, his eyebrows rose and his eyes widened further. He seemed to be in a mixture of shock and pain.

'You are the last Thistlewick Thespian,' Becky continued.

The old man opened and closed his mouth several times, as if trying to find the right response.

'I don't need reminding,' he said, and his voice was suddenly cracked with emotion.

'Sorry,' Becky said.

'How did you…?' Cyril's words trailed off.

'I found Emily's diary.'

'Emily's… where?'

'In the Secret Theatre.'

There was a long silence, during which Cyril stared at Becky and Jimmy shifted nervously beside her.

'What do you want from me?' Cyril finally said.

'Theatre sounds amazing and the Secret Theatre is beautiful,' Becky said, choosing her words carefully. 'I would like to put on a new production there, but the problem is I don't know much about theatre, and no one else on Thistlewick will help because theatre's supposed to be banned.'

Cyril stared around the room and then the pained expression returned to his face. He put his head in his hands.

'Sorry,' Becky said again.

Maybe she had said too much. She guessed he hadn't heard the word 'theatre' coming from the mouth of someone else for many years.

'It causes me great pain to think back to what happened,' said Cyril at last, his head still lowered. 'And I do not want to talk about it now. Please, leave me.'

Becky felt very sad for the old man, but was also worried that he would never want to help. Then she had an idea. Opening her bag, she took out the diary and looked around the room for a place she could put it. She settled on the bedside cabinet.

'I'll leave Emily's diary here.'

It was difficult to leave the diary behind, as she wanted desperately to continue reading it, but she felt it was important. Perhaps the diary would remind Cyril what theatre was like, or if he had never forgotten, it would show him how much he used to enjoy it. She hoped he'd look at it.

'Come on, Jimmy.'

Jimmy, who had been staring uncertainly at Cyril, walked out of the room, and as Becky reached the door, she looked back one final time to Cyril, who was staring at his drawn curtains again, before closing the door behind her.

***

Becky jumped as she walked through the front door.

'Where have you been?' Her mum was standing directly in front of her, a very cross look on her face.

'Just out,' Becky replied.

'I've had people complaining about you. First Sergeant Radley, and then Mrs Didsbury, saying you were asking about events in our past that you shouldn't even know about. After everything we went through the other day with Midsummer House, did it not cross your mind that there's a reason you haven't been taught about certain things?'

'No.'

'Well, I've had enough. You're grounded for the rest of the week.'

CHAPTER 14
Betrayal

Becky felt terrible.

In her diary, Emily had described Cyril as a great actor with a big smile, and he certainly had a big, contented smile in the photo of the Thespians that Becky kept looking at. It must have been Albert and the Renegade Group who had turned him into who he was today. The thought that they had taken away the happiness of such a talented person by banning theatre all those years ago made Becky angry, and also left her with a dilemma.

She wanted now, more than ever, to bring the theatre back to life and put on a production, to prove to the rest of the island that it shouldn't be banned. But she wasn't sure how this would be possible without Cyril's help.

What's more, she hadn't been allowed out of the house, apart from to go on postal errands, for the last four days, and her mum didn't look like she would ever give in with her grounding.

Becky had no diary and no Cyril. Was there no hope?

***

On Friday afternoon, while she lay on her bed with her hand on her head, Becky heard the doorbell ring. It wouldn't be for her, though.

But then she heard two pairs of footsteps coming up the stairs, and her door opened.

'Becky, you have a visitor,' said her mum.

Jimmy stepped into the room.

'You're free to go out now,' her mum continued. 'As long as you promise to behave yourself.'

'Yes, Mum.'

Her mum walked out, leaving Jimmy standing inside the door.

'Nice shorts,' Becky said. He was wearing bright red ones – with a picture of a space rocket sewn onto the pocket.

'Thanks, they're new.'

'It's really good to see you. I've been going mad in here.'

'I told the others about what happened with Cyril,' said Jimmy.

'Will said. So what are we going to do?'

'I don't know. But Ben and Harriet think it'll help if we can find out why theatre was banned.'

'How, though? We've tried everything.'

'I've got to return this book to the library.' Jimmy held out *Thistlewick: the Timeline*. 'I thought we could go and have another hunt around in there.'

***

Becky stood with her hands on her hips in the cramped attic room of the library.

'It's no good, Jimmy, we've looked on all three floors, and there's nothing.'

Jimmy turned around from the ancient bookcase he was searching through and sighed. 'Let me have one last look up here. You never know.'

Becky moved over to the chair by the window and stared bleakly around the room. As Jimmy shuffled past her, she spotted something opposite – a section they hadn't even considered looking in.

'Jimmy, do you think there could be information in that old newspaper rack?' She walked over to it. 'Even if there are no books about the Renegade Group, there are bound to be articles in a newspaper about them.'

They walked over. The sign on the rack read: *Back issues of The Chronicles of Thistlewick. Handle with care.*

Becky flicked through a few of the papers nearest to her. 'It looks like there's one paper each month. What date did you say the Renegade Group came to Thistlewick?'

'They came in January nineteen fifty-two and left in September that year.'

'Let's find the newspapers for that time.'

Becky ran her hand along the long line of papers and, stopping halfway along, pulled one out.

'December, nineteen forty-three,' she read. 'Too early.'

She pulled another one out a bit further on.

'November nineteen fifty-one. We're getting closer.'

She was about to put the paper back, but then she saw the photo on the front cover.

'Look, Jimmy, it's the same photo of the Thespians that I have. And look at the title.'

CYRIL SILVERDALE PUTS IN STAR PERFORMANCE

The island of Thistlewick was treated to another exceptional production by the Thistlewick Thespians this month. And one actor stood out in particular.

'Cyril did a remarkable job considering this was his first production,' said head of the Thespians, Emily Wilson. 'I'm so proud of him.'

The production, which was written by Emily and performed over two nights at Thistlewick Church, was called *The Knights of Kingdom Rock* and followed the story of a shipwrecked sailor-boy who becomes stranded on an island full of old knights.

'I am not only proud that our island has such a talented group of performers,' said head of the island council, Philip Castle. 'I am proud to be a member of that group.'

We look forward to seeing a new production from

the Thistlewick Thespians next year, but will have to wait to find out what it's about.

'All I will say is that it involves a paintbrush,' said Emily.

'That would have been *The Magic Paintbrush*, Jimmy.'

'Thistlewickians clearly loved theatre before the Renegade Group came, then,' he replied.

'And so did Cyril,' Becky said sadly, thinking of the old man sitting in the darkened room. 'So if that was November nineteen fifty-one, a couple of papers along should be for the month the Renegade Group came to the island.'

Her hand shaking slightly, Becky pulled the paper out.

'Oh… it's for October nineteen fifty-two. That's just after the Renegade Group left.'

'So there obviously weren't any newspapers when they were here,' said Jimmy.

'This is no good, then,' Becky said, disappointed. 'We've got no hope of finding anything out if there's not even a newspaper from that time.'

'Hang on,' said Jimmy. 'Look at the headline on that October paper.'

Becky looked down and read:

DRAMATIC BETRAYAL LEADS NEW HEAD OF COUNCIL TO KEEP ONE OF RENEGADE'S RULES

It is hard to believe that only last month our island was in the grasp of the evil man Renegade. Now that he has left our shores, we are starting to pick up the pieces, and hopefully our new council leader, Albert Gailsborough, will guide us in doing so.

'Albert became council leader!' Becky said. 'How could they let that happen?'

But today, dramatic news has reached us: Two Thistlewickians betrayed us and joined the Renegade Group. It is, of course, common knowledge that Ralph Little was seen by several people signing a contract with Renegade.

'That was bad enough', says our new leader, Mr Gailsborough, who was Ralph's best friend. 'But I can tell you now that there was in fact another person who betrayed us. Emily Wilson'.

Becky's eyes widened, and her breathing got faster as she continued reading.

According to several eyewitnesses, Emily was seen leaving Thistlewick with Ralph in Renegade's own boat.

What makes this more heartbreaking is that both Ralph and Emily were Thistlewick Thespians.

'We used to love theatre', said Mr Gailsborough. 'But then Renegade came along and banned it. For a while Emily and Ralph fought against him with the rest of us – there was even a rumour they were building a theatre in secret. But now they have betrayed us by joining the evil man and his organisation. I'm in complete shock.'

Renegade imposed many rules on Thistlewick Island, all of which our newly elected council leader has undone – except one.

'Because the betrayal was by two Thistlewick Thespians, Emily and Ralph, I can only assume that it was linked to theatre in some way. Therefore, I am maintaining the ban of theatre on Thistlewick Island.'

Becky couldn't read any more.

'So Albert wasn't a member of the Renegade Group,' said Jimmy. 'He fought against them like everyone else.'

'But how could he think that Emily betrayed Thistlewick?' Becky asked.

She felt a tear running down her face. It didn't make any sense. In Emily's diary she had talked passionately about her fight *against* Renegade. It couldn't all be lies.

'There's no way she would have joined the Renegade Group.'

'But what about her being seen with Ralph Little? They both went off in Renegade's boat,' Jimmy pointed out.

'Well this Ralph may have betrayed Thistlewick, but how could Emily? I... I just don't get it.'

'At least we know why theatre is still banned, though,' said Jimmy. 'If Albert thinks the Thistlewick Thespians betrayed the island, that's why he won't let you even say the word "theatre".'

Chapter 15
A Letter for Becky

Becky tried to hide her tears that evening as she sorted through the post ready for the Saturday morning rounds.

'Mr R Fairbanks, Wigfield Cottage, Thistlewick.' She placed the large envelope into the delivery basket.

She really was confused. First, she had thought Albert was a member of the Renegade Group and now, according to the paper, it turned out Emily had been.

'Mrs D Standen, Clifftop House, Thistlewick.' This letter carried the smell of a sickly perfume, and she quickly threw it to one side.

It had all been going so well, and now she didn't know what to think or do. She desperately needed to see Cyril to find out the truth; but if she went to him now, maybe it would cause him more pain. Perhaps she should wait, but Becky wasn't very good at waiting.

In frustration, she screwed up the envelope she had just picked up, then instantly regretted doing so. Getting angry with the post wouldn't solve anything. She unscrewed the envelope and read the address.

Miss Rebecca Evans
The Post Office
Thistlewick

She reread the wispy writing in surprise.

Who's this from?

She dug her fingernail into the seal and tore open the envelope. Lifting out the plain sheet of paper she read:

Dear Becky,

Thank you for coming to see me earlier this week. I'm sorry I was so grumpy, it's simply that what you said took me completely by surprise. I never imagined someone of your generation would use the word 'theatre', let alone tell me that they discovered the Secret Theatre, after what happened all those years ago. I have now read Emily's diary and would like you to come to see me again, if I didn't put you off the first time.

Kind regards,
Cyril

Becky jumped up and ran out of the post office, abandoning the big pile of post still to be sorted.

As she shot through the market in the fading light, past the stall tenders packing up after their day's work, she wondered what had changed to make Cyril contact her.

***

'Go on through!' Pat Galway called to Becky as she ran into the bar of the White Wing Pub and Hotel. 'I don't know what you said to Cyril the other day, but he's changed quite remarkably!'

When Becky arrived outside room seventy-three, she knocked on the door excitedly. This time there was an immediate response. When Cyril opened the door, Becky almost didn't recognise him – his face was full of life and his eyes didn't have a dead look in them now; in fact they were glowing, and Becky realised they were bright blue, just like hers.

'Hello, Becky,' he said, almost out of breath. He seemed as excited as she was.

'Hello, Mr Silverdale.'

'Please, call me Cyril. Come in, come in.'

Cyril held the door open for her and she walked into his room. Even though it was dark outside, Becky noticed that his curtains were open.

'I'd forgotten what a lovely view that was,' he said. Becky turned round to face him. 'It was wonderful watching the sun setting over the sea this evening. Do sit yourself down.'

He indicated his bed and Becky sat down on the edge of it as he moved over to his chair. She noticed one other change in the room – the red box that had been by the chair had now moved onto the bedside cabinet, and its lid was slightly ajar. Becky wondered what was in it.

'Did you get my letter?' asked Cyril. His voice was gentle and warm.

'Yes.'

'Good, good. I'm sorry for being so short with you last time. No one has dared to speak to me about theatre for many years and, as I explained, I certainly wasn't expecting a young girl like you to do so.'

'You said you've read the diary?' Becky asked.

'Yes, I have, all of it. Thank you so much for leaving it with me.' Cyril beamed at her.

'What's made you so happy?' She couldn't help herself asking – the change in him was incredible.

'It's Emily. She didn't betray Thistlewick! I always knew she didn't, but the diary confirmed it.'

Becky looked at him, puzzled. 'I don't understand.'

'You haven't read to the end of the diary, have you?'

'No, I haven't got that far into it,' Becky admitted.

'You must read it. The final entry.'

He jumped up as quickly as his legs would allow and presented Becky with the diary.

'Turn right to the end,' he said. 'To the final entry.'

CHAPTER 16
Emily's Final Words

3rd September 1952

So much anger has built up inside me over the last few weeks. The Renegade Group have been more cruel than I ever thought possible. Only last Tuesday they locked my fellow Thespian Bernie in a cage because he had dropped a pail of water. The poor man is eighty years old, for pity's sake! My anger increased so much that I decided to act on it two days ago. I had had enough!

I thought through all the ways I could protest against Renegade. Which would be most effective? Which would show him my love for theatre? I have tried protesting before: taking a stand at work on the farms, or outside his headquarters, but it has never worked. No, this time I needed something special.

September was approaching and I realised the first day of the month would be the perfect time to protest, for on this day Roden's Rock would appear. It shows itself only once a year to the west of our shores for a few hours, and the people of Thistlewick treat this event with great respect and wonder.

This, I decided, was where I would take my stand.

So on that morning, I made my way over to Roden's Rock, early enough to slip past the guards on the shoreline. I walked onto the rock and started my protest: I chose a scene from The Magic Paintbrush and acted it out for all to hear. The experience was like magic, and soon lots of people stopped to watch me, but it was shortlived. A guard spotted me, and a large group of Renegade's men headed out towards me in boats. I jumped off the rock and swam. I swam until I was out of sight, then fled back here to Midsummer House.

I know they will come for me now. They have done before. The first time I protested they locked me up in a cupboard in Renegade's own house; the second time they caged me in the forest and deprived me of food and water. After that they gave me a final warning – if I protested again I would face grave consequences. So I know they are coming, and I know this will be my final fight.

I have spent the last few days preparing the Secret Theatre, making safe all the things that need to be protected. I do so hope they won't find the theatre. After all the effort and time my group of Thespians have given to our cause, I wish with all my heart that it isn't taken from us because of my foolish protests.

I have sat here for several hours now thinking back through all the happy memories I share with the Thistlewick Thespians, before and after 'they' arrived. I wouldn't have missed any of what we have done for the world, let alone for such an evil man as Renegade.

I hear a knocking. It's coming from the front door. 'They' are here. My time has come. I know I cannot defeat them, for they are too powerful. But I will fight. I will fight them with my whole life for everything I believe in, to the end.

The knocking is getting louder — it's more like thunder now. I must finish this entry here, for I am ready to leave my theatre in peace. I may return to write further entries, although I doubt it.

But now I must go to meet the Renegade Group.

'You see?' asked Cyril, as Becky lifted her head slowly. 'Emily continued fighting. She didn't give in to them. She didn't betray Thistlewick.'

'But she was seen going off in a boat with the Renegade Group,' Becky said.

'She wasn't going with them of her own will. She tried to fight – the diary proves that – but they were too powerful. She had been the thorn in their sides for a long time, and so they captured her and took her away with them when they left. Poor Emily.'

'What about Ralph, the other Thespian? He was seen signing a contract with Renegade.'

'I don't know if he betrayed us or not. In truth, I can't remember much about him, just that he was a quiet man.'

'Maybe he was captured with Emily?'

'Perhaps. Oh, poor Emily. To think of her being taken away from what she loved the most, from her dreams; and they probably ruined her beautiful home too – the Renegade Group did that sort of thing, you know, they tore all the furniture out and took away any life a place had, leaving it to rot.'

That explains the large piles of broken furniture at Midsummer House, Becky thought.

'If only I could have been there for her.' Cyril turned away to look out of the window, and Becky could tell he was crying.

'You couldn't have done anything,' she said softly. 'But Emily didn't give in, she fought to the end.'

Cyril breathed in deeply and turned back round, his eyes shining with tears. 'Yes, she did. Emily did us proud.'

'Why didn't you all continue fighting?' Becky asked. 'The Thistlewick Thespians I mean. Surely you didn't believe that Emily had betrayed you?'

'The loss of Emily tore us apart, and there was a lot of confusion. Some of the Thespians took Albert's side and believed his story of betrayal. When Albert was elected as the new council leader, that was the final straw. He banned theatre and kicked Philip Castle, who had been a Thespeian, off the council. Albert never really trusted him, or any of the Thespians, again. As for me, I didn't know what to think. I never truly believed Emily had betrayed us, but I was young, Becky, I let Albert's words get to me, and I ended up accepting his story. Now, looking back,

I've lived a dull life and let myself waste away. But maybe that's about to change, now that you've discovered the theatre.'

'No one else believes me about it,' Becky said. 'Apart from a few of my friends.'

'Of course no one thinks you're telling the truth, Becky, they're still afraid to mention the word "theatre". No one on the island knew about the Secret Theatre apart from the Thespians, and with theatre still being banned, no one has dared to go searching for it – until you came along.'

'I want to put on a production at the Secret Theatre,' Becky said. 'I want to show people that they shouldn't be scared of theatre, and now I know the truth I want to carry on Emily's fight.'

Cyril's eyes lit up. 'Oh Becky, what a wonderful idea! Is that with your friends?'

'Yes. But there's one problem. I don't know how to put on a production, none of us do. Will you help us?'

Cyril smiled, and as he spoke another tear ran down his cheek. 'Becky, I'd love to.'

CHAPTER 17

The New Thistlewick Thespians

Things started to take off the following week, when all the children, or the New Thistlewick Thespians as Becky called them, met at the theatre.

Watching them file into the stalls, Becky realised she had mixed feelings about the others being in the theatre. It was fantastic to know that they were about to start a production, but a few days ago the Secret Theatre had been just that – her secret. She wasn't completely happy about fourteen other people knowing it existed, apart from Cyril, of course, who was standing at the front and hadn't stopped smiling since they'd arrived.

'Right,' he said. 'I'd like everyone to move up onto the stage, please.'

'How are we all going to fit up there?' asked Jack.

This was a good point. Becky couldn't see how all

fifteen of them could be on the stage at once. It might have been quite long, but there was only about a metre of space between the big red curtain at the back and the edge of the stage.

'Come with me, young man, and I'll show you how we can make it bigger,' said Cyril.

He gestured to Jack, who followed him nonchalantly up onto the stage. They disappeared behind the curtain.

Becky still wasn't sure why there was a big red curtain there – it seemed odd, because curtains usually covered windows, and Becky didn't think there was a huge window behind this curtain. But as everyone waited to see what Cyril and Jack were doing, it all became clear to her.

The curtain began to divide into two parts and moved to the sides of the stage, and as Becky looked on, quite astonished, she saw that the stage extended far back behind where the curtains were, about seven or eight feet. It had never occurred to her that there was more space *behind* the curtains.

'This whole area is where you perform,' Cyril said, appearing from one side with Jack, who looked quite impressed. 'The curtains close at the front so that the set can be changed between scenes without the audience seeing. Ok, everyone up!'

Cyril spent the rest of the morning showing the children what acting was, and they all had a go at playing different characters. Becky played everyone from a posh millionaire to a downtrodden servant.

Jack caused them all to laugh a lot when he got bored

with being a policeman and ran around the stage as a monkey. Despite it not being what he was meant to do, Cyril did say that Jack's monkey impression was a good example of acting.

'That was really challenging,' Becky said to Jimmy as they sat back down in the stalls an hour later. 'But so much fun!'

'Yes,' said Jimmy quietly.

Becky looked to her friend – he didn't seem that happy. He'd been having a good time up on stage, so what was wrong with him now?

'Let's have a chat about the production,' said Cyril from the front. 'I understand you've decided which characters each of you will be playing in *The Magic Paintbrush*, so we can go on from there. It will take us about two months to prepare for a final performance.'

'Two months! That's a long time,' said Jack.

'We've got a lot of work to do,' said Cyril.

'Who will we be performing to?' asked Harriet.

'Hopefully, it will be to a lot of Thistlewickians. We'll need to get over the fact that theatre is currently banned, but we can worry about that later.'

'My mum's going to be really excited about this,' Isabel announced to everyone.

'Don't be stupid,' said William. 'We can't tell anyone what we're doing now.'

'Why not?' asked Isabel.

'You heard what people on Thistlewick think of theatre,' said Ben. 'If they knew we were coming here, they'd try to stop us.'

Out of the corner of her eye, Becky saw Jimmy raise his hand.

'Yes, Jimmy?' asked Cyril.

'I don't think I'm comfortable about not telling my mum. She asks me what I've done each day and I keep having to make things up.'

'Ok. Well, if you really feel uncomfortable, it's perfectly fine for you to pull out now,' said Cyril. 'No one would think badly of you.'

Becky stared at her friend, hoping he wouldn't want to stop – he was meant to be the main character; who else would be able to play Andrew?

'Is it ok if I see how it goes?' asked Jimmy.

'Of course,' said Cyril. 'But we do need to tread very carefully. We cannot talk about this to anyone outside the theatre. Albert is leader of the council and he's responsible for maintaining the ban on theatre. He knows everyone on Thistlewick, so if word gets out, he'll find out easily. Now, in my opinion, theatre is one of the greatest things you can be part of – it can transform you, just wait and see. A few days ago I was slumped in a chair with no life left in me, and then Becky told me about the Secret Theatre. Look at me now.'

Becky smiled as she listened to Cyril – the change in him had been incredible.

'It's a risk, but our best bet will be to work on our production and discover the joy of theatre for ourselves. Then we can try to show the islanders. Albert is stubborn, but if we can prove to everyone else how good theatre is, he may just give in.'

CHAPTER 18

Becky's First Rehearsal

The sun was shining brightly as Becky walked along the coastal path the following week, and she enjoyed the warmth and the sound of the sea lapping against the shoreline.

The New Thistlewick Thespians had spent a lot of time in the last week reading through *The Magic Paintbrush* and preparing their characters. Becky's Queen would be powerful and scare all in her presence, and she had been working on it in front of her mirror for the last few nights.

One night, her mum had unexpectedly walked into her room just as Becky was shouting, 'Off with her head!' Fortunately her mum hadn't realised exactly why Becky was saying this, and just laughed.

Today was Becky's first rehearsal. Jimmy had had one two days before, where he went through the first scene of the play with Cyril. His character, Andrew, who wasn't very good at art, discovered a magic paintbrush, which allowed him to paint perfectly when using it.

Becky still wasn't sure if Jimmy was going to carry on with the production or not – he had changed the subject when she'd last asked.

But she tried to clear her mind of these thoughts and concentrate on her character.

Powerful and scary. Powerful and scary!

As she passed by the harbour, she saw Albert hobbling with some effort up the path towards her. She tried to prepare herself for what he might say.

'You haven't been to Midsummer House again have you, young girl?' he asked, almost accusingly, but also with a lot of concern.

'No,' Becky lied.

'You promise?'

'Yes,' she replied shortly. They had all agreed to keep it a secret, and she was more than happy to do so – especially from Albert. Even though she now knew he wasn't part of the Renegade Group, he was still nearly as bad as far as Becky was concerned – how could he think that Emily had betrayed Thistlewick and ban theatre because of it?

'Good,' he said. 'And you must never go there again. Midsummer House is a dang'rous place, associated with things you shouldn't know about. Now, I do remember what I was like when I was your age, many years ago – I always wanted to go out explorin'. That's fine, it's part of bein' young, but some things are forbidden for a reason, and you must…'

But Becky didn't really hear the rest of what Albert said, because she had just seen Ted coming out of the harbour hut and moving over to a barrel of fish.

Your father was a Thistlewick Thespian, she thought. *Philip Castle, he helped to build the Secret Theatre. I wonder if you know that.*

Ted looked up to the path, and, seeing Becky with Albert, smiled. He started to sort through the barrel and Becky thought of Ted's own son.

Now Jack Castle is a Thistlewick Thespian.

'…so, if you need somewhere to create adventures, find another place to explore. Understand?' Albert seemed to have finished his lecture.

Becky turned back and looked at him vaguely. 'Yes.'

Obviously satisfied that he'd got his message across, Albert nodded at her and returned to the harbour to help Ted sort through the fish, and Becky went back to thinking about her first rehearsal.

***

When she got to the theatre later that morning, she was surprised to see all fourteen of her friends there. She found out from William that they had all turned up to see how she did as Queen.

'Right, let's begin,' said Cyril. 'Becky, if you'd like to position yourself up on stage, and Issie, if you could prepare to go up with the painting.'

At the start of Becky's first scene, scene three, she had to sit to one side of the stage and stare out into the audience, looking menacing. In the final production she would have a throne, but for now, when she walked up onto the stage, full of confidence, she took a normal chair from the left-hand wing.

'Are you ready, Becky?' asked Cyril.

Chapter 19

The Frightened Queen

As she turned around to face Cyril and everyone else sitting around the stalls, she felt very alone, and now with fourteen sets of eyes staring up at her expectantly, she suddenly became very nervous.

'I'd like you to start by staring out into the audience, and then Issie will walk onto stage and speak to you, ok, Becky?' Even though Becky knew that Cyril's voice was kind and quiet, she had still heard his words as if a ferocious lion had roared them.

'Er… y-yes,' she said.

Becky stared out into the audience. She became more and more scared with every passing second.

The Queen is meant to be scary, Becky, not scared, she thought.

'Becky.'

She jumped at the sound of Cyril's voice.

'It's your line,' he said.

Looking round, Becky saw Isabel, playing her maid, next to her, holding a piece of cardboard, which would be a painting in the final production.

She opened her mouth, but as she tried to speak, nothing came out.

It wasn't that she had forgotten her words, because she knew them off by heart; it felt more like she'd forgotten how to speak. Inside her head she shouted out her first sentence.

But this is a feeble painting, how dare you show me such rubbish!

But all she could manage out loud was a mumbled, 'But... er... I...'

After what seemed like hours, Cyril said, 'Are you ok, Becky?'

'I... er...' She started to panic, and as she looked down into the audience, each pair of eyes became predators staring up at their prey. 'No.'

How could she have been so confident about what she was doing? How could she have spent all that time practising, and not be able to say a single line now?

'Shall we try again?' Cyril suggested. 'Let's start with you staring out into the audience.'

Becky looked up slightly, but she still felt like a frightened rabbit. A tear slowly trickled down her cheek and she closed her eyes.

The next thing she felt was a hand on her shoulder and she heard Cyril say, 'It's alright, Becky, come with me.'

When she opened her eyes again, she was in the library, with Cyril smiling at her.

'Why couldn't I do it?' she asked, her voice shaking.

'I think you got a touch of stage fright, Becky,' he replied.

'Stage fright?'

'It's when you get nervous standing up on stage, sometimes so much that it feels like you can't speak.'

'That's how I just felt,' Becky admitted. 'But why? I've stood up on stage before and been fine.'

'Yes, but in the acting workshop you were working in groups, not on your own in front of an audience. Sometimes it feels like the audience, even if they are only your friends, are your worst enemies – like their eyes are staring at you fiercely, as if they want you to fail.'

It had felt like this to Becky too. Cyril was right – without having to do it in front of an audience she was fine, and the first time she had stood on the stage when she had discovered the theatre, she had looked confidently out over the empty seats. It was only when they were filled that Becky couldn't act.

'But why was it only me?' Becky asked. 'Isabel didn't get stage fright.'

'A lot of people have it, on different levels. I was like you when I had my first ever rehearsal. When I stood up in front of Emily and the other Thespians, hundreds of butterflies seemed to be fluttering around my stomach and my heart was replaced by a drum – I got stage fright.'

'But you obviously weren't affected like I was, because you became a really good actor. How can I ever be good at acting if it's like that every time I do it in front of people?' She was nearly in tears.

'Becky, you expect too much of yourself. I know you've spent hours performing in front of your mirror, but in front of people it's very different, and it was a completely new experience for you. The good news is that you can conquer your stage fright, and it was Emily who helped me with mine. During that first rehearsal she saw I was struggling, so she took me to one side and gave me some advice.'

He knelt down so that he was at the same height as Becky, and gave her a warm look.

'Emily told me that everyone gets nervous. If you don't, then you're just not human. But you can use those nerves to your advantage. The heavy beat of that drum in your heart is what will give you the power to reach out to the whole theatre with your voice, and those butterflies, they will float out one by one with every word that you say. And if it's the audience who are scaring you, then you just have to shut them out. Instead of seeing lots of people staring at you, try to imagine that it's just you, standing in front of your mirror. Close your eyes if you have to, and only open them after you've said a few lines and are more confident.'

'But I can't close my eyes every time I'm on stage. People will think I'm weird.'

'No, of course you can't, but at least it will get you through this first rehearsal. We can work more on your stage fright in the coming weeks. So, come and have another go. You just have to think positively and remember Emily's advice.'

Becky wasn't sure if she had the courage to go back in. She still felt pathetic about her first attempt and wanted to ask Cyril to let her do the rehearsal when no one else was there, but then everyone would think she was a coward.

She thought back to all the time she had spent practising at home and how determined she'd been to get it right. If she didn't go back in now, all that effort would have been wasted. Becky took a deep breath and walked back into the theatre.

As she moved through the stalls the rest of the children were silent. She felt them staring at her and looked straight ahead to the stage. She began to shake and felt the *thud*, *thud*, *thud* of her heart beating faster as she walked up the steps.

She turned around to face the audience. It just felt like they were all laughing at her as she struggled. Becky closed her eyes and tried to think of Emily's advice.

'Scene three,' came Cyril's voice. This time he sounded like the Cyril Becky knew – kind and gentle. 'Off we go.'

I can do it, I won't make a mistake! Nerves are good. I can use them to help me.

She kept her eyes shut.

'Here is the painting, your majesty,' said Isabel.

'But this is a feeble painting. How dare you show me such rubbish! Have the painter beheaded. Bring me a new painter tomorrow – a good one.'

Becky could hear the shake in her own voice and knew that it cancelled out all the power she was trying to show. But she had managed to say her first line!

She opened her eyes. Trying to ignore the audience, she stared straight at Isabel. It seemed to work, and she continued with the rest of the scene.

CHAPTER 20

The Costume Cupboard

When Becky walked into the Secret Theatre for her next rehearsal a few days later, she found William and Jimmy chatting in the stalls and Harriet in conversation with Cyril.

'And what are those two golden masks meant to represent?' asked Harriet, pointing up at the happy and sad faces above the stage.

'I can answer that,' Becky said, and both Harriet and Cyril turned to face her. 'I read about them in Emily's diary the other night. The masks are a symbol of theatre. They were first used in Ancient Greece thousands of years ago, when actors wore them to show what their character was like. There were lots of masks showing lots of different emotions, but the main ones were a smiling mask, showing a happy character, and a frowning mask, showing an unhappy character.'

'There was also an evil mask,' said Cyril. 'Back in Ancient Greece it was said to suck the soul out of anyone who looked at it. Masks haven't really been used for centuries, but they still represent how theatre started. Anyway, Becky, come with me'

Beck followed Cyril up onto the stage and into the backstage area.

Cyril took a packet of matches out of his pocket and lit a candle – there was no electricity backstage, so everything had to be done by candlelight.

This was an area Becky hadn't explored properly yet. In the flickering light of the candle she saw thick wooden floorboards leading on one side to a big wooden screen separating backstage from the main stage, and on the other side to a few doors. It had quite a dusty atmosphere and there were odd pieces of furniture, papier-mâché rocks and two fake trees scattered around it.

'Props from past productions,' Cyril explained. 'We built those trees for the original production of *The Magic Paintbrush*. Now, the door in front of us leads to the costume and props cupboard. I think that if we find the Queen's costume it might help you to get more into character and release some of your nerves.'

He held the candle close to the door.

'Go on, Becky, you open it.'

Becky placed her hand on the doorknob in great excitement – every time she opened a door at Midsummer House she discovered something new. The door swung open.

'Oh!' Becky and Cyril both said, almost at the same time.

The cupboard was empty. There wasn't a single dress or tunic anywhere to be seen, let alone any props, unless you counted the old broomstick in the corner.

'Where has everything gone?' said Cyril, quite taken aback. 'Can you see anything, Becky?'

He waved the candle around the room. As the light hit the far corner, Becky noticed something white lying under the broom.

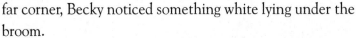

'It's a piece of paper,' she said, walking over to it.

'Is there anything written on it?' asked Cyril.

Becky picked it up, and recognised Emily's handwriting. 'Only a date – the thirty-first of August, nineteen fifty-two.'

'I wonder what Emily's trying to say. That must mean something – she wouldn't have left a single piece of paper in an empty room without reason.'

'Maybe it's linked to the diary?' Becky suggested. As always, she had it close by, and pulled it out of her bag.

'What happened on that date?' asked Cyril.

'It was the day before Emily's protest on Roden's Rock.' Becky started flicking through to find the right entry.

'Of course!' exclaimed Cyril. 'Knowing that she was taking that risk the following day on Roden's Rock, and that the Renegade Group would soon come for her, she would have moved everything that was valuable to another location. There must be something hidden in that diary entry!'

'I can't find anything,' Becky said. 'The only thing that's odd is that there's half a page which is blank. There's no writing on it.'

'Aha!' Becky had never seen Cyril so excited. 'Hand me the diary.'

Becky did, and to her alarm he held out the page that was half blank and placed the lit candle under it!

'What are you doing?'

'Invisible ink!' said Cyril.

'What?'

'Mix orange juice with water and you get invisible ink! You write with it, and it can't be seen on any paper. Until, that is, you heat it up!'

Sure enough, as he spoke, two words appeared in the empty space on the page, in dark brown letters.

The Globe.

'Yes! I remember Emily telling us about this. In one of the toilets in Midsummer House is a painting of the Globe Theatre, one of the most famous theatres in the world. The props must be hidden somewhere near it! But which toilet could it be?'

'I think I know,' Becky said. 'Come on!'

She dashed out of the cupboard, through the curtain and off the stage, Cyril trying his best to keep up.

'What are you…?' began William as Becky rushed past him.

'It's hidden… in the toilet!' Becky replied.

She ran out of the theatre and through the library into the entrance hall, Cyril and the others following behind. Remembering the ancient toilet she had discovered on her first trip to Midsummer House, Becky shot across the hall and pushed the stiff door open.

'Is there a painting on the wall?' asked Cyril, catching up and handing the candle to her.

She shone it around the room. There was nothing on the left hand wall, or the back, but on her right was a small painting of a circular building.

'Is that it?'

'Yes, that's the Globe,' said Cyril, his voice bristling with excitement.

'What's special about a painting of this Globe?' asked William, standing in the doorway.

In answer, Cyril walked over to it, placed a hand on either side of the frame and lifted it down off the wall. In the space where it had hung was a lever.

'Another secret door!' Becky said.

'William, can you do the honours,' said Cyril.

'Of course!' William stepped forward and pulled down hard on the lever. It clicked outwards and there was a small rumble from the other side of the wall, but nothing moved – no secret door was revealed.

'Now what?' asked William.

'Is there anything else in the diary entry, Becky?' asked Cyril.

'I don't think so.'

'There's still space at the bottom of the page. Try waving the candle under it again. Not too close, mind.'

Becky held out the diary page with the words 'The Globe' written on it and carefully placed the candle underneath. At first nothing happened, but then another word slowly appeared at the bottom of the page.

'Flush!' Becky called out.

'What?' asked William, and Becky heard Harriet giggle from outside.

'It just says "Flush",' she said.

'Try giving the toilet a flush, then,' said Cyril.

Becky looked at the toilet uncertainly. It was the sort where you had to pull a chain from above to flush it. She grabbed hold of the chain.

'Here we go.'

She pulled down.

Nothing.

'Try again,' said Cyril. 'It's been a long time since that toilet was used.'

Becky pulled the chain again. This time a rumbling noise came from the toilet's cistern and soon water was splashing down into the toilet bowl.

'Whoa!' said William.

Becky turned around, and saw the left hand wall sliding away.

'A false wall,' said Cyril.

As it disappeared, a light clicked on in the gap and another room was revealed.

'Look at it all!' Cyril stared ahead in wonder.

Becky stepped forwards. The room was packed with all sorts of different items: several racks of costumes, including dresses, knights' armour and pirate outfits; there were hats and wigs in a box; scattered on the ground were everything from fake flowers to model trains to alarm clocks.

'Every prop and costume we ever had. These are the true treasures of the Secret Theatre.' said Cyril. 'And look here.' He knelt down and picked up a long object.

'Jimmy, it's your magic paintbrush!' Becky exclaimed.

'I wonder if it's really magic,' said Jimmy.

'I doubt it,' said William.

'But there's no harm in trying.' said Cyril.

'Can we find the Queen's outfit?' Becky asked.

'It'll take me a while to sort through everything in here, so I'll try to find it for you another day. I hope it'll fit – many of the costumes we have here will be too big for you lot.' Cyril looked at Becky. 'I think the Queen's outfit should fit you, though. Emily was quite small. In fact, I've just spotted the shoes she wore.'

He bent down and took a pair of pearly white shoes out of a box. Intricate floral patterns were woven along them, broken up by shining beads.

'Try these on, Becky.'

She knelt down and took her own shoes off.

'I have tiny feet,' she said.

'So did Emily,' replied Cyril, handing her the Queen's shoes.

Becky placed one in front of each of her feet and stepped into them. To her surprise, they fitted perfectly.

'Wow! I have the same sized feet as Emily!'

'Why don't you keep hold of them for now, and as I said, we'll sort costumes out at a later date,' said Cyril. 'Right, let's get back to the theatre.'

Becky turned around towards the entrance.

'AAAAHHHH!'

She had had the scare of her life. William and Jimmy were standing there, but their heads had been replaced by two golden masks!

'Pretty cool, aren't they?' came William's voice. He lifted the mask, revealing his grinning face behind it. 'We found a box full of them.'

'You scared me!' Becky said.

'I must say I got a bit of a shock there as well,' said Cyril.

Becky saw that William had been wearing a mask with a miserable face; Jimmy was still wearing his mask, which was staring at her with a fixed grin.

'Take it off, Jimmy, that's really creepy!'

CHAPTER 21

The Secret Theatre was in darkness as Becky entered. No longer could she see the beautiful reds and golds.

What have I come here for?

She walked forwards, feeling her way along to the front row, and sat down in one of the seats.

The theatre was in complete silence. Becky started to shiver – as far as she could tell, she was in her pyjamas.

Suddenly a distant sound reverberated, like the stamping of hordes of feet. It got faster and faster. The feet started to stamp in rhythm, like the beating of a big drum. Louder and louder. The chandelier above her started to rattle with the vibration.

What's going on?

As quickly as the sound had started, it stopped. The theatre returned to silence. Then, through the darkness, a face suddenly appeared. A golden mask. It was a long way away, but shone so brightly it almost blinded Becky.

Another golden mask appeared next to it.

'Jimmy, William, is that you?' Becky called out. Maybe they were playing a trick on her.

No voices responded. But the masks both turned sharply to face her. With a jolt, she saw that these masks didn't have happy or sad faces; theirs were evil. Cruel grins and raised eyebrows.

She remembered Cyril's words: *'There was also an evil mask… said to suck the soul out of anyone who looked at it.'*

The blank holes of the masks' eyes suddenly started to change and were now glowing bright red. That meant only one thing to Becky – danger.

'Help! Help!' she tried to scream. But nothing came out.

There was an explosion of light and as it cleared, the stamping started again, but this time much closer.

In front of her were many black-cloaked figures dancing around the stage, and all the while their golden-masked faces seemed to be locked onto Becky.

She didn't know what to do.

Then she heard another noise. It came faintly at first, because the stamping was so loud.

'Help me, Becky! Help me, Becky!'

Soon it became clearer.

'Help me, Becky! Help me, Becky!'

Instinctively she knew who the voice belonged to.

'Where are you, Emily?'

Then she saw someone, at the centre of the masked figures. It was a woman, cowering on the ground, her long dress flowing around her.

'Help me, Becky! Help me, Becky!' the woman called.

'I'm coming, Emily, I'm coming!'

Becky stood up and ran towards the steps leading to the stage and the ring of cloaked figures. As she climbed the first step, she felt her heart rate increase, and step by step it got faster and faster. Then she realised her heart was beating in exact time with the stamping.

As she reached the final step the stamping stopped. Her own heartbeat stopped too. The masked figures all turned to face her and she couldn't breathe.

Through the figures, she could just see Emily and tried to focus on her. Her face wasn't happy now like in the photos; it was scared, her eyes blinded with fear.

The stamping started again. So did Becky's heart. But this time the golden masked figures were moving towards her. They began to chant.

'Be-cky!'

'Help me, Becky!' came Emily's voice.

'Be-cky!'

The figures were getting closer, surrounding her on all sides.

'*Be-cky!*'

'Help me, Becky!'

'*Be-cky!*'

The stamping and chanting got faster and faster. One of the golden masks drew closer still.

'*Be-cky!*'

It was so close now that Becky could see the terror in her own eyes reflected in its golden surface.

'*Be-cky! Be-cky!*'

The mask got bigger. Suddenly it was twice the size of her, its evil face glaring down.

'*Be-cky! Be-cky!*'

'Help me, Becky!'

'*Be-cky!*'

The mask moved forwards. It was about to swallow her.

'BE-CKY!'

It wrapped its mouth around her. All the sounds became one long, unbearable scream. And then…

Darkness.

Silence.

'Becky! Becky!'

She felt herself being shaken. She opened her eyes and sat up with a jolt as she saw her mum and brother sitting on her bed. Her mum had her hand on Becky's shoulder and looked very worried.

'Becky, are you ok?'

'What was… where…?' Becky stammered.

'You were having a nightmare, love, that's all.'

'But I…'

'Will heard you from next door and came to fetch me. You were shaking quite violently.'

Becky glanced towards her brother. He didn't have his usually smirking grin on his face – he too looked worried.

'Sorry,' Becky said.

'Don't worry,' he replied quietly.

'You've obviously been doing too much lately,' her mum said. 'I think you need to take it a bit easier, so a few days of rest will do you good. I'll go and make you a hot drink and Will'll stay here to keep an eye on you.'

Her mum got up and walked out of the room.

Becky stared at her brother. 'I was at the Secret Theatre.'

'You probably should calm down a bit, Becky. A lot has happened to you recently,' he said.

She looked down at her hands. They were clenched in two tight fists.

It was true, she had been through a lot in the past few weeks. Perhaps it had all suddenly caught up with her.

Or had she *really* seen Emily?

Part 2

CHAPTER 22
Jack

Becky skipped along the path leading northwards, humming a happy tune as she went.

It was the first week of August and the winds were picking up around Thistlewick, as they always did at this time of year. But today the blue sky wasn't troubled by any clouds, and the sun didn't have to fight to cast its warm rays of light across the island.

This was the first time Becky's mum had let her out of the house since her nightmare the week before.

It had all been quite frustrating – in an effort to make her relax, her mum had insisted that she spent most of her time in the living room, listening to music or reading a book. Of course, Becky couldn't have brought Emily's diary into the living room and had to settle for reading the various storybooks lying around the house, all the while thinking about how she could turn them into pieces of theatre.

Usually she would have wanted to play outside with her friends at the weekend, but today she was heading straight for Midsummer House. She desperately wanted to read the diary again, and she missed being in the theatre on her own.

William had told Becky that in her absence, the boys, led by Jack, had started to build the set for *The Magic Paintbrush*, using materials they'd found in the costume cupboard. Becky was curious to see what it looked like.

As she pulled out the book in the library and the shelf slid out of the way, the door to the Secret Theatre was revealed. But as she approached it, Becky sensed there was something different about the door.

But what is it? she asked herself.

Then she realised – there was light coming through the cracks around the edge of it.

That's odd.

Usually the lights in the theatre only turned on when you opened the door.

Is someone already in there?

She turned the handle and walked through. The first thing she saw was the stage, and she noticed a ladder resting against one of the columns, which hadn't been there before. At the top of the ladder was Jack.

Becky froze. She was always a bit nervous around Jack – he was older than her and could be a bit bullish. But what was he doing here? She saw that he had a hammer in his hand and was banging it into the column – he was obviously working on the set. As he drew the hammer away from the column, he turned to face Becky.

'Oh, hi,' he said, and waved to her.

She smiled back at him slightly and was about to say 'hello' when something dreadful happened.

As if in slow motion, Jack lost his footing and with one hand holding the hammer and the other waving at Becky, he began to fall. Becky saw his expression change to panic, but there was nothing he could do as his foot became trapped between two rungs of the ladder. Becky ran towards the stage as fast as she could, but before she reached it he had landed on the floor with a sickening thud. The ladder came crashing down on top of him.

The sounds echoed around the theatre for a long time, and when they finally cleared there was a deathly silence.

'Jack, are you ok?'

There was no reply.

She climbed up the steps to the stage, her heart in her mouth. Jack lay in a crumpled heap on the floor, the ladder across his stomach. With a great effort, Becky lifted it off him, hoping it hadn't broken any of his bones.

'Can you hear me?'

She knelt down over him. His eyes were closed and a thin trickle of blood was running out of his nose and down his cheek.

'Jack! Oh no, what can I do?'

She knew she shouldn't leave him alone in the theatre, but what other option did she have? She had to get help.

Becky got to her feet and ran out of the theatre.

Who can I tell?

Trying to control her panic, she realised the only person it would be safe to find was Cyril.

She ran through the garden gate and as fast as she could down the track. By the time she reached the stile leading to the Market Square, she had a painful stitch in her side, but she had to keep going. Then, in the distance, she saw Cyril walking towards her.

After what felt like several minutes, he arrived at the stile.

'Hello Becky, it's good to see you out and about again. I'm on my way to the theatre. Is that where you've just come from? What's wrong?'

'It's Jack, he's fallen… in the theatre!'

***

Jack lay, stiller than still, surrounded by white sheets and pillows. Cyril was looking anxiously down at him, his hand on his head. Becky stood next to him in the back room of the doctor's surgery.

Jack didn't look any better, but at least the doctor had cleared the blood from around his nose. Apart from this, a few bruises and a twisted ankle, no physical damage had been done, and they were now waiting for him to wake up to make sure everything else was ok.

The door opened briefly and Dr Crystal appeared.

'Mr Castle is here to see his son.'

Her head vanished and the door closed again.

Becky looked straight to Cyril. 'We can't tell him what happened!' she said. 'We can't tell him about the theatre!'

'Becky, we have to. Whether it's good or bad for the theatre, we have to do what's right.'

Becky didn't have time to argue back, because as Cyril finished talking, another voice came from behind them.

'Hello,' said Ted Castle.

They didn't say a word as the fisherman walked slowly over to the bed and knelt down beside his son.

Becky couldn't stop herself from shaking. It had all been going so well that she had almost forgotten about the islanders' opposition to Midsummer House and the idea of theatre. Now that opposition was dangerously close to finding out the truth.

After a few moments, Ted turned to Cyril.

'At least he ain't too badly hurt. What on earth happened to him?'

'Ted, why don't you sit down?' said Cyril.

And he told the fisherman the whole story, about the theatre and everything they had been doing. Becky watched as Ted's face slowly whitened, and she expected him to jump up and start shouting at them – that's what her mum would have done. But he didn't, and as Cyril finished Ted just sat in silence, staring at Jack.

After a very uncomfortable five minutes, Becky began to wish Ted had reacted angrily. At least then she would have known how he felt. Now she didn't have a clue and that was almost worse.

Eventually Ted turned away from his son.

'I really don't know what to say,' he said quietly. 'I can't agree with what you've been doin'. Theatre is banned on Thistlewick, you know that, Cyril.'

'The theatre's really great, Dad.'

At the sound of Jack's voice, they all turned around to face him. He had obviously just woken up and was squinting around at them.

'Jack, thank goodness you're safe!' said Ted, and he put his arms around his son in a tight hug.

'The theatre is really great,' Jack repeated.

'But what you've been doin' ain't right, son,' his dad replied. 'I'm goin' to have to tell the council.'

'No, Dad,' said Jack, sitting up in bed. 'Don't you see? You can't tell anyone – if you do they'll try to stop us, and you can't let that happen, we're in the middle of a production.'

Becky smiled at Jack – she hadn't known he'd felt that way. She had thought that because he only had a small role in the production and wasn't as keen on acting, he wasn't enjoying being in the theatre as much.

Ted puffed out his cheeks. 'Well, if that's really how you feel, then I'm willin' to give it a chance for you, Jack.'

Becky breathed a sigh of relief.

Ted continued. 'But it's a big thing for me to be doin', goin' against the council like this. I can't be certain about it until I've seen a rehearsal.'

Becky wondered how Ted knew the word 'rehearsal'. Then she remembered – his father had been a Thistlewick Thespian. Maybe Ted knew quite a bit about theatre.

'You can help us with the set, Dad.'

'Yes, I think that would be an excellent idea,' said Cyril. 'We could do with someone to supervise set building, especially after what happened today.'

'Alright, I'll come along to a rehearsal next week – Jack'll tell me when. And I won't tell no one about all this before then.'

'Right,' said Cyril, sounding quite anxious. 'And Becky, Jack, you need to promise me you won't return to the theatre again alone.'

'I promise,' Becky said.

They all looked to Jack to see if he would promise as well, but the only sound that came from him was a long snore – he was fast asleep.

***

The rest of the house was in silence as Becky sat up in bed. Her mum and brother had been asleep for what felt like a few hours now. She couldn't get to sleep, however hard she tried, and was chewing a chocolate bar thoughtfully.

What will happen if Ted doesn't like what we're doing? Will he tell the council? What will happen if he does?

No matter how many times she went over these questions, her mind couldn't find an answer.

But what she did know was that the fate of the Secret Theatre, and a lot else, rested on Ted's visit the following week.

CHAPTER 23

The Balcony

'In the play so far, the main character, Andrew, has found a magic paintbrush, and when he uses it he can paint wonderful portraits, which impress the Lords and Ladies around his kingdom,' Cyril explained to Ted. 'In the next scene, Andrew is painting Lord and Lady Thickwistle. Ok, off you go, Jimmy.'

'Good evening, my Lord, my Lady,' said Jimmy, bowing courteously.

'Enter,' said Ben, playing Lord Thickwistle. 'Won't shake your hand. Probably covered in paint, what!'

The scene proceeded and Jimmy acted out Andrew's painting of the Thickwistles.

Becky really admired Jimmy's acting. He was able to show his character's emotions so well that for a second she almost forgot he was Jimmy, her friend, and thought she really was watching a person called Andrew. It was also incredible that for such a shy and nervous boy, he could stand on stage with so much confidence– something that Becky still struggled with. She just hoped that he would continue with the production – he'd said very little to her about how he felt.

As Andrew finished the painting, Lord and Lady Thickwistle moved over to look at it.

'Oh, isn't it wonderful, dear?' trilled Lady Thickwistle, played by Harriet.

'We shall tell all our royal friends about you, young man,' said her husband.

'Excellent. Ok, so Andrew goes off stage right,' said Cyril, and Jimmy followed his instruction. 'Now we would have a blackout.'

Becky was trying to figure out what a blackout was when she heard Ted's voice and turned sharply to face him. He had sat quietly next to Cyril throughout the rehearsal and Becky hadn't been able to tell whether the expression on his face was a good or bad sign.

'...brilliant. This is so much fun! The children are doin' really well, aren't they?' he was saying.

So she needn't have worried – Ted liked what they were doing. That meant the theatre was safe, for now at least.

Cyril smiled.

'Right,' he said. 'Scene six. As Andrew is building his reputation as an artist, the Queen of the land continues to behead artists for painting portraits of her that she dislikes. Can I have all the characters for scene six up on stage, please.'

Becky climbed onto the stage and took a chair out of the right wing – her throne was still being built.

She sat down on the stage and took a deep breath. She thought about what Cyril had said a few weeks before:

'Remember, you're the Queen. The people around you should feel nervous in your presence, not the other way round!'

They had worked together on how she could turn her own nervous feeling when she was on stage into the Queen's power. She tried to focus on doing this now.

'Ok, off we go,' said Cyril.

Becky watched as an artist, played by Jack, made a feeble effort to paint her. After a while she thought the Queen should become bored, so she started to look around the stage, then gazed out into the audience. As she did, she saw something up in the balcony. It was a person sitting in the front row.

'Finished!'

She turned around to face Jack, who was holding the painting up to show her.

'Bring it here,' she said distractedly.

As he walked over to her, she glanced back to the balcony, and… there was no one there. But she knew she had seen someone. A woman. Emily?

Jack coughed and placed the painting in front of her.

She realised she was shaking – how could Emily have been in the balcony? She tried her best to stay in character for the rest of the scene.

'A feeble painting. The worst yet. Behead him!'

'No, your majesty, don't do that,' said Jack as he was dragged off stage.

'And next time bring me a decent artist. All my friends speak of a boy called Andrew. Bring him to my castle to paint my portrait.'

***

'Are you alright, Becky?' asked Cyril at the end of the rehearsal. 'You seemed a bit dazed up on stage. It's not the nerves playing up again, is it?'

'I think I saw Emily, up in the balcony,' she replied.

'Are you sure?'

'Yes, there was definitely a woman.'

'Right, let's head up there, then. Ted, could you come and help us?' asked Cyril.

'I'd be delighted to,' the fisherman replied.

'We'll also need a few more helping hands, so Jack, Jimmy, Ben and Harriet, you come too.'

'Why do we need so many of the others?' asked Becky.

'We've got a lot of work to do if we want to get up to the balcony,' replied Cyril.

***

'So it's up those stairs?' asked Ben.

'Yes, the balcony can only be accessed from up there,' said Cyril.

They were standing in the entrance hall of Midsummer House, at the bottom of the grand marble staircase that Becky had climbed up on her first visit.

'We've got to get past all that junk, then?' asked Jack.

'All the furniture will have to be moved, yes.'

'Let's get going, then!' said Ben.

Cyril managed to rig a torch up to the banister so they had more light to work in, and piece by piece they moved all the furniture off the staircase. Becky worked with Jimmy and between them they lifted down two armchairs, a big mirror and a small table.

'Come on,' Becky said fifteen minutes later, when all the furniture had been removed.

Eight pairs of footsteps echoed through the entrance hall as they all ran up the staircase and across the landing.

'Through the door on your left, Becky,' called Cyril.

She flew straight into the door and it swung open, causing her to stumble through into the room. She caught her balance on a small bed.

'This was Emily's guest room,' explained Cyril.

'I can't see a door anywhere for the balcony,' said William.

'The bookcase!' Becky exclaimed, for on the right hand wall of the room was a small bookcase with books that looked similar to the ones in the library downstairs. 'We have to find the book about theatre.'

'This secret entrance is a bit more of a challenge to reveal,' said Cyril.

'Do you know how?' asked William.

'Oh yes, in fact I came up with the idea for this one. But it will be a challenge for you.'

'Aha!' Becky said. 'Here it is. A *Concise History Of Theatre.*'

She pulled the book out, but unlike the one in the library, which got stuck halfway, this one came out easily, and nothing happened.

'I told you it would be a challenge,' Cyril said with a smile. 'Try looking in the space on the shelf where that book was.'

Becky squinted into the gap, and there, on the back wall of the bookcase, was writing.

'Two right,' she called out.

There was a short silence as they all thought about what the words meant.

'Maybe you pull the book out that's two to the right of where that book was,' suggested Harriet.

Becky did, and behind *The Stargazer's Annual, 1950* was another message.

'Bottom, five in!'

She bent down to the bottom shelf, counted five books in from the left and pulled out *Lord Thistlewick: Now and Then.*

'Nothing, there's no writing at the back.'

'Maybe it means five in from the other end,' said Harriet, and she bent down and pulled out the fifth book from the right. 'Got it. It says: top, twelve in.'

Becky stretched her hand up, but definitely couldn't reach the top shelf.

'Jack, could you do it?' she asked.

Jack stepped forwards, casually counted twelve along and, reaching up, plucked *The Unlocked Door – a crime novel* off the top shelf. But as he did it got stuck – he couldn't pull it more than halfway out.

'This is it!' Becky said.

The bookcase slowly slid out of the way, leaving a small gap in the wall, which lead to... the balcony!

Becky stepped through and glanced around.

'Anyone there?' asked Cyril.

'No,' she replied.

'When we were rehearsing for the original production of *The Magic Paintbrush*, Emily used to sit in the front row of the balcony to watch us,' Cyril explained to the others as Becky walked down to the front row.

All the seats in the theatre were known as 'tip-ups', because when someone wasn't sitting in one, the seat part would 'tip up' against its back. People hadn't used the balcony seats for over fifty years, so they were all folded up. As Becky moved to the front, though, she saw one with the seat down. It was as if someone had only just got up from it.

Becky saw something on the seat and picked it up. It was a golden badge and on it were the familiar masks of the happy and sad faces.

'Is everything alright down there, Becky?' Cyril called.

'Fine,' she replied.

She carefully folded the seat up against its back and walked up to join the others.

***

'This is the badge that Emily used to wear all the time to show her belief in theatre,' said Cyril, turning it around in his hand.

'That's a bit scary,' said Harriet. 'Becky sees someone in the seat Emily always used to sit in, then she finds Emily's badge lying on it.'

'Maybe it's a sign,' said Ben.

'A sign of what, though?' Becky asked.

'It's a good sign, I think,' said Ted. 'It could show that Emily's spirit is with you, that she's supporting what you're doing.'

CHAPTER 24
Garden Trouble

The following Monday the New Thistlewick Thespians found themselves in the garden of Midsummer House.

After they had cleared all the objects from the staircase, Harriet had suggested that they should make Midsummer House look more welcoming, so that people wouldn't be as worried about going there.

'We need to tidy it up, especially the garden,' she had said.

Most of the boys were pulling up weeds and creating a brand new vegetable patch, while some of the girls were preparing new plants to go in the de-weeded areas. Jimmy was repainting the sign welcoming people to Midsummer House and Becky was clearing the path of leaves.

'I'm still not sure that working in the garden of Midsummer House is a wise thing to do,' Cyril said. He finished tying up a bag of dead leaves and placed it in a rusty bin he'd found. 'It feels very open. If someone sees us here it could be quite awkward.'

'But we're not actually inside the house, so they can't complain about that,' Becky said. 'And if anyone comes and asks why we're here, we can tell them our planned excuse.'

She stopped raking the leaves for a moment and thought about their excuse – she hoped it was good enough.

She looked out of the garden and over the surrounding landscape. The sky was grey and overcast, which made everything seem lifeless. No one would walk this far from the main part of the island with the threat of rain, so they should be safe.

As she bent down to untangle a few leaves from her rake, Becky noticed a bird sitting on the branch next to her – it was the same goldfinch she had seen in the garden before. She smiled and it tweeted at her, puffing out its yellow breast. As she continued her job, the bird stayed by her side and occasionally its merry song would brighten up the cold August day where the sun failed to.

Just like Emily's smile, Becky thought. *That would have brightened up the day.*

'In fact, that's a good name for you,' she said to the bird. 'I'll call you Emily.'

After an hour of hard work, the garden was beginning to look, if not beautiful, then certainly a lot tidier.

Cyril stood up and winced. 'I shouldn't be doing this sort of work at my age.' He still had a smile on his face, though. 'How are you getting on, Jimmy?'

'Fine, thanks. I've just got one more word to repaint.'

'So, are you sure you want to carry on with the production now?' asked Cyril.

Becky looked up.

'Yes,' said Jimmy. 'I'm having so much fun. Mum isn't asking as many questions now, either, and I've decided that not telling her will make it a really good surprise when she sees the final production.'

He glanced over to Becky and gave her a small smile, which she returned.

'That's a lovely thought,' said Cyril. 'Well, I'm glad you're staying, Jimmy. You're doing really well in the production.'

'Yes, you are,' Becky said.

Jimmy returned to his work, concentrating hard on writing each letter on the sign in exactly the same way that Emily had done.

Cyril bent down to Becky and whispered, 'Jimmy reminds me of myself when I was his age. When he first came to see me with you, Becky, he didn't say a word, because he was too nervous around me, but up on stage he really comes to life.'

Becky nodded.

'That's just what I was like when I started acting,' Cyril continued. 'Being a Thespian really helped to increase my confidence, so I hope it can do the same for Jimmy.'

Cyril looked off into the distance, past the garden gate, and then his expression changed to a frown. Becky followed his gaze.

'Oh no!'

Up the faded path, Albert the fisherman was walking determinedly, followed closely by Ted. As he arrived at the other side of the gate, the work in the garden seemed to stop, as everyone stared at Albert in an uncomfortable silence. He stood about a metre away from the gate and wouldn't step any nearer.

'I saw you in here from my boat. What on earth are you doin' at Midsummer House?'

All of a sudden Emily the bird, who had been so devoted to Becky, flapped her small wings and flew away – she disliked the accusing tone of Albert's voice as much as Becky did.

'I told you,' said Ted. 'They're makin' it look presentable.'

'One of the reasons this place worries folk is because of its abandoned appearance,' said Cyril.

'There's a good reason that Midsummer House is abandoned, as well you know, Cyril Silverdale,' Albert argued back.

Even with all his wrinkles, Becky could tell that the fisherman's face was tense.

'We're not actually *in* Midsummer House,' she said.

'Oh, aye,' said Albert stiffly.

'Look, the children are doing a summer project on gardening and they needed a garden to tidy up. All the other gardens on the island are beautifully kept, so we thought we would give this one the same treatment – stop it from being a sight that looks out of place on Thistlewick,' said Cyril.

'This place caused great harm to our island.'

'It didn't, Albert, it's just a building. It was never used by the Renegade Group.'

Albert flinched at Cyril's mention of Renegade.

'Besides,' Cyril continued, 'they moved on long ago, and you can't tell us that there are supporters of that group still living on Thistlewick.'

'Well, we don't know. There are some groups of people who are still under suspicion,' Albert said meaningfully, glaring at Cyril. 'You're all comin' dang'rously close to breakin' a law of our island. I suggest you move away from here this very moment.'

With a final glare at Cyril, then at Becky, the fisherman turned around and walked away as fast as his old legs would carry him.

Once he was a good distance from Midsummer House, Ted moved forwards and leaned over the gate.

'I'm sorry about Albie, he's stubborn in his ways. Perhaps it was a bit of a risk comin' out here. If you'd told me your plans I would have warned you that today is Albie's day for fishin' off this part of the island.'

'Well, at least he didn't react too badly,' said Cyril.

'Did he believe us, about the garden?' asked Becky.

'I think so, lass, I think so,' said Ted. 'Now, listen up. I was over on the mainland the other day pickin' up some nets, and I happened to walk past the Theatre Royal. I would have avoided it before, but this time I was curious, so I went to see what production they had on. It's a play called *A Royal Undertakin'*.'

'Oh, I enjoyed that when I was a boy,' said Cyril with a beaming smile.

'Would you like to see it again?' asked Ted.

'I would love to.'

'Good, 'cause I booked tickets to go and see it on Friday mornin'.'

'For all of us?' asked Becky.

'For all of you,' replied Ted.

CHAPTER 25
A Royal Undertaking

'*The Theatre Royal: Where the Best Plays Are Shown!*' the sign outside the theatre proclaimed.

It was the sort of grand building that had clearly been used for many years, but this only added to its atmosphere – Becky could feel its history living and breathing around her. There were quite a few people moving past the six marble columns that held up the front of the building, mainly retired men and women, dressed very properly in suits and long dresses. They walked through large doors into what Cyril explained was called the 'foyer'.

Ted handed each of the children their own ticket and they started filing through, showing the tickets to a man dressed in a smart blue suit. Looking at her ticket, Becky was delighted to see that she was in 'Seat 12, Row A, Grand Circle'.

'You all need to head up those stairs on the left,' the blue-suited man said to them.

When Becky entered the Grand Circle she looked over the edge at the theatre around her. It had the same sort of effect on her as the Secret Theatre – just as beautiful, just as powerful – but it was quite a bit bigger. The Grand Circle was the balcony above the stalls, and there was another balcony above it that Becky had seen was called the Second Circle. The theatre had just as much gold around it as the Secret Theatre, but instead of lots of red, it had mainly blue colours – blue carpet, blue chairs and a magnificent blue curtain stretching across the stage. Above the stage, where the golden masks were at the Secret Theatre, there was a statue of a man and a woman, standing in very dramatic poses.

Becky shuffled along the front row and found her seat, next to a plump old man dressed in a smart suit and slightly wonky bow tie. As she sat down beside him, she saw that he had a very merry face with bright, rosy cheeks.

The theatre was buzzing with the chat of all the audience members, waiting for the performance. Becky stared around in fascination – would the audience at the Secret Theatre be like this, as they waited for *The Magic Paintbrush* to start?

'Is this your first trip to the Theatre Royal?'

Becky turned to face the old man.

'Yes,' she replied. 'In fact, it's my first time seeing a performance at all.'

'Well, you're in for a treat. This is a good 'un.' He had a deep voice, which was almost a continuous chuckle. 'My name's Henry Smith.'

He leant towards Becky and held out his hand.

'Becky Evans,' she replied, shaking it.

'It's my granddaughter's first time at the theatre too.'

Becky glanced past him and saw a young, curly-haired girl in a very pretty dress, sucking her thumb and staring in awe at the people around her.

'She's only five, bless her,' Henry said proudly. 'Her name's Bethie.'

'Hello, Bethie.'

The girl turned to face Becky and took her thumb out of her mouth, revealing a cute grin.

'She's rather excited,' Henry added. 'I've been here many times myself. A seasoned pro, I am. Lovely place, great shows. Nothing beats a live performance.' He fiddled with his bow tie, making it even more wonky. 'So why have you come here today? I take it you're on a trip with your friends?'

'Yes. We're putting on our own production called *The Magic Paintbrush* by Emily Wilson, and Ted – he's a fisherman – he bought us tickets for this so that we can see how a professional theatre works.'

'Well I never! Putting on a play when you haven't even seen one before! Fascinating.' He chuckled. 'You certainly have the enthusiasm for it.'

Becky smiled at him. She started to look around the theatre again, studying all the people in the stalls below and wondering what they most enjoyed about coming to the theatre.

'I bet you can't see a single row in the stalls down there that doesn't have a bald man in it,' said Henry.

Becky looked along each row in turn, and couldn't help but laugh as she saw that in most rows there were actually several men who didn't have any hair on the top of their heads.

'It's always the case. Every time I sit up here, I see a bald man in every row. In fact, baldness is one of the reasons I now sit in the Grand Circle – I don't want anyone staring down at my bald head.'

Becky took the smile off her face. Perhaps she shouldn't have laughed at the people below – it wasn't their fault they didn't have hair.

'As my hairline has receded, so has my position in the audience!' Henry snorted.

Becky didn't really understand what he meant, but his reaction put the smile back on her face – he was such a jolly man!

'Oh, here we go,' he said.

Becky turned to face the stage. The chatter of the audience died down and the theatre was suddenly plunged into darkness. Becky felt a tingle run down her spine – the performance was about to begin! A beam of light lit up the centre of the stage as the curtains opened. A man dressed as an undertaker was standing over a grave. The rest of the stage was in darkness.

'Oh, what a day today was meant to be.'

His voice was loud and clear and even from a distance Becky could see the sorrow on his face. He looked down at the gravestone.

'But alas it's a sad one, for you, and for me. My princess, Rachel, who I so wish to wed, is locked in her father's castle, left for dead.'

More light shone on the stage as the man turned around. Behind him, a backdrop was revealed, painted to show more gravestones leading up to a hill, on which a large castle sat.

'Daylight,' he said.

As the play continued Becky became more and more involved in it. At every scene change she felt a shiver of excitement at what would come in the next scene, and as each new character was introduced, her heartbeat increased. It felt so real – as if it were actually happening there in front of her.

In the third scene, the King was introduced. He was a giant man with a big, red beard, but his personality was exactly the same as that of the Queen that Becky would be playing. She studied the actor's performance closely. He used a loud, booming voice and had a look on his face that made Becky think he was going to explode. She truly believed he was an evil, angry leader.

At the half-time interval Henry turned to Becky again. 'Good, isn't it?'

'It's amazing!'

'They're a fine set of actors as well. Brian Blakely – the man playing the King. I've met him in the past. As shy as a mouse in real life. You wouldn't think it, would you, the way he acts on stage?'

'No,' Becky replied.

If Brian Blakely can act that scarily, then so can I, she thought.

'So what do you think will happen in act two?' asked Henry.

'I think the undertaker will rescue the princess and then they'll kill the King,' Becky replied.

'Interesting theory. Well, we shall see.'

'Granddaddy.'

'Yes, my love?' said Henry, turning towards Bethie on his other side.

She was bouncing up and down in her seat.

'Oh, I see,' he said. 'You want to go to the little girls' room, do you?'

He got up and squeezed his way along the row, his granddaughter following behind.

I wonder what Bethie thinks of the play, Becky thought.

Someone tapped her on the shoulder, and she turned around. Most of the others were sitting in the row behind her.

'It's really good, isn't it?' said Harriet.

Becky grinned at her. 'Yep.'

As the lights came up on stage for act two, Becky made a point of studying Bethie's reactions. The act started with the King sending his guards to search for the undertaker. Bethie jumped slightly every time he raised his voice and sucked her thumb nervously.

Does she think he's a real person? Becky wondered.

Maybe to Bethie the play was really happening; maybe she thought the characters actually existed. Becky knew that if she had been five, she would believe what was happening on stage.

In the next scene, where the undertaker tried to rescue the princess, Bethie's big eyes were fixed on him. She was on the edge of her seat and her hands lay in her lap, her thumb forgotten. When the undertaker was discovered by the guards and he nearly failed, it looked like Bethie wanted to jump down onto the stage to help him.

The young girl's reactions proved to Becky just how powerful an experience theatre was and reminded her of her own first reaction to seeing the Secret Theatre.

The play finished with the King being taken to prison, followed by the undertaker and princess getting married and becoming King and Queen.

At the end all the actors took bows at the front of the stage and the audience clapped for them. A boo was let out for the King and a cheer for the undertaker and princess – everyone had clearly enjoyed it.

'Well, it was lovely to meet you, Becky,' said Henry as he stood up to leave. 'And I hope your production goes well.'

'Thank you. Did Bethie enjoy the play?'

'Well, Bethie, did you?' asked Henry.

His granddaughter replied with a big nod.

As Becky made her way out of the theatre, her friends chatting animatedly around her, she thought one thing.

It's exactly how Emily described it!

CHAPTER 26

Destroyed!

'...so seeing *A Royal Undertaking* has certainly given me confidence that we're on the right lines with *The Magic Paintbrush*,' said Cyril.

Me too, Becky thought.

'Before we start today's rehearsal, there's another matter we need to address,' Cyril continued. 'As we're now coming to the end of August, we need to think about how we're going to get the islanders along to see the play.'

'Perhaps we could make some posters?' suggested Isabel.

'It's a good idea, Issie, and were we holding a bring-and-buy sale that would be fine. But on this occasion posters just won't work. If the people who are against Midsummer House find out about it they'll try to stop us before we have a chance to show them anything.'

'So we have to find a way to get people along without actually telling them where or what it is they're coming to?' asked William.

'Exactly,' said Cyril. 'That's where our problem lies. We've got a bit of time on our side, but I'd like everyone to rack their brains and come up with some ideas for how we can advertise our play... without advertising it, if you know what I mean.'

As he stepped down from the stage, the door to the theatre opened.

'Oh, hello, Ted. We weren't expecting you today.'

Becky turned around. Ted walked into the theatre and stood at the back, breathing heavily – he had clearly just been running.

'We have a problem,' he said. 'I've just been to an emergency council meetin', which Albert arranged.'

Becky instantly knew something was wrong – Ted never called his fishing partner 'Albert', he always referred to him as 'Albie'.

'It must be something quite serious?' said Cyril. 'The last time an emergency council meeting was called was to arrange the arrest of Tristan Traiton last year.'

'It was about Midsummer House.'

'Oh.'

Becky closed her eyes. Had they been found out?

'Tell us the bad news,' said Cyril.

'It's been agreed that Midsummer House should be destroyed.'

'Destroyed!' Becky called out.

All of the children started murmuring to each other.

'Why?' asked Cyril.

'It was what you told Albie about tidyin' the garden. You said the house doesn't fit in with the rest of the island. That stuck in his mind, so much so that he decided to take action. And the council agree with him – Midsummer House should be knocked down.'

Becky started to shake. She wanted to go and shout at Albert, to tell him what he had just done.

'They can't do that. If they destroy Midsummer House, they'll destroy everything we've worked for, and everything Emily and the Thistlewick Thespians worked for!' Becky felt tears of anger and sadness running down her cheeks.

Ted looked at her sympathetically. 'I think we have a chance to save it, Becky. It'll take them a good while to get ev'rythin' sorted. I'd say we have at least a month.'

'So our performance will happen before they destroy Midsummer House?' asked Becky.

'Yes, Becky, that's right,' said Ted. 'So what we have to do is encourage the whole island to come here and see the play. Then they might understand the good that you're all doin', and that this place can't be knocked down.'

'But how do we get everyone to come, when they want to destroy Midsummer House?' asked Becky.

'That's a very good question,' replied Ted.

'And one we can't seem to answer,' said Cyril gravely.

***

'Becky.'

Becky turned around and saw Ted beckoning her.

After his news no one had felt like doing any proper practice. What they had planned as a rehearsal of scene eight, where Andrew's paintbrush was stolen as he journeyed across a dark forest to get to the Queen's castle, had fizzled out into a read-through of a few scenes. When it was her turn, Becky had read her lines as if they were out of a maths textbook.

'Yes, Ted?'

'Jack and me would like you to come for tea at our cottage tonight.'

'Um… ok.' Becky couldn't think why she had received the invitation. She and Jack weren't exactly good friends – they had hardly spoken to each other since his accident.

'We'll see you at six, then,' said Ted, then he leant down close to her ear and whispered. 'We have something you might be interested in seein'.'

CHAPTER 27

The Secret in the Boat Shed

At six o'clock Becky found the Castles' front door wide open.

'Hello?' she called.

'Come on through. I'm in the office,' came Ted's voice.

Becky walked into the low-ceilinged hallway, and through a door into a small dining room. The main feature of the room was a large oak table, which could seat at least ten people. The Castles were famous for their dinner parties and regularly covered the table with amazing fish pies and pasties. The last time Becky had been here was for Jack's birthday party last year when everyone had come dressed as a type of fish. Glancing around, she saw a photo from this event hanging on the wall, among a large collection of stuffed fish.

She had always imagined a fisherman's house would be like this, but she'd never thought it would contain an office like the one she saw through the door in front of her.

Ted was crouching down, looking through the bottom drawer of a cupboard. When Becky walked into the room she saw a large desk with neatly arranged files of paper positioned around it. There was a formal chair and a stand with a telephone on it.

Ted looked up and obviously read the expression on her face.

'I manage the money for the fishin' fleet, so I need the office to keep ev'rythin' in order. Anyway, Jack's clearin' a few things out in the boat shed, and we'll go out there in a minute, but I wanted to show you somethin' first.'

Becky looked down at what Ted was holding. It was a black and white photo of a man dressed in a knight's outfit.

'Is that your dad?'

'Aye, it is. I've got a few photos of the Thistlewick Thespians in here.'

He handed her the photo and reached in to pick another one out of the drawer.

'They're from a production called *The Knights of Kingdom Rock*.'

'I read about it in an old newspaper. It was the last one they did before the Renegade Group came, wasn't it?'

'That's right. I remember my father tellin' me some crackin' stories about it. They used to be so busy durin' a production that he never had the time to mend his nets at work. My mum wouldn't let him bring them home, so on the nights the Thespians were performin' he used to sit at the side of the stage when he wasn't on and mend his nets.'

Ted chuckled as he looked at a copy of the same photo of the Thespians that was at Midsummer House. His eyes were shining brightly, as if reliving his memories.

'Have you always known about the Secret Theatre?' Becky asked.

Ted continued looking at the photo for a few seconds, then glanced up at her. 'Aye, I have. My father told me all about it when it was bein' built. It was our secret.'

Becky bent down next to him. 'Why didn't you tell them at the council meeting I came to? No one would listen to me, but you knew.'

'It had been in the past for so long, and it was always our secret. After Emily had gone, my father never really talked about it again. Not with me anyway. I don't think he dared to after it was banned and he was kicked off the council. So I thought it was best to keep it in the past. Besides, if I'd told Albie about it that would've been a great shock to him.'

As Ted spoke, Becky realised how much affection he had for his fellow fisherman.

'Why is he still so against theatre? Everything with the Renegade Group happened over fifty years ago.'

Ted puffed out his cheeks in thought. 'Well, Becky, he's a stubborn old fellow is our Albie. He fully believes that his friend, Ralph, and Emily both betrayed Thistlewick, and his grudge against them is as strong now as it ever was.'

'Do *you* think Emily betrayed Thistlewick?' Becky asked.

'No. My father never thought she did. I believe she kept on fighting and loved this island to the end. That incident with the badge in the balcony proved it for me. As for Ralph, maybe he did betray us, but I certainly don't think it was the theatre that turned him against Thistlewick. There's no tellin' Albie that, though.'

Becky nodded sadly.

'Now, come with me,' said Ted. 'And I'll show you my shed.'

***

The boat shed next to Ted's house was a large wooden structure capable of housing a full-sized fishing boat. It was a mishmash of old and new wood, as if it had been standing there for hundreds of years and various generations of the Castle family had hammered on new planks to stop it falling down.

As they stepped inside, the smell of seaweed and dead fish hit Becky powerfully. There was a light on in the far corner, where she could see Jack shifting boxes, but apart from this it was dark.

'I don't use it much,' said Ted. 'My boat's better off at

the harbour. It rusts if it sits in here for too long.'

He flicked on a torch and guided Becky past the boat-launching ramp to the back of the shed.

'How's it goin', son?'

As his voice echoed around the shed, it was muffled by the dampness, unlike the clear, crisp sound of echoes in the theatre.

'Yeah, fine. Lots of boxes,' replied Jack. He was wearing rough jeans and an old shirt with lots of holes in it.

'A few more boxes and we're there, I think,' said Ted.

He helped Jack with the remaining cardboard boxes, moving them over to a new pile Jack had made.

'And here we have it,' said Ted, simultaneously pointing to the ground with his left hand and shining the torch at it with his right.

Becky saw a patch of the wood, a few feet wide, which was separated from the rest of the floor around it – a trap door.

'This, Becky, is a tunnel. A tunnel that used to lead to the Secret Theatre.'

Becky barely noticed her mouth falling open. Ted bent down and with a great effort lifted the trap door, revealing a deep, dark abyss beneath.

'That's amazing, Dad. How come you never told me about it before?' asked Jack.

'It was a secret. Like the theatre, your grandpa told me never to tell anyone about it.'

Becky knelt down and squinted into the hole. 'Is this how your dad got everything to the Secret Theatre when the Thespians were building it?'

'Spot on, Becky. It was too dang'rous to do it over ground in case the Renegade Group saw him. So at night he would go out in his boat, collect the materials and bring them back here. Then he would carry them along the tunnel to the theatre – I think it comes up under where the stage is.'

'Could we use this to get people to come to the theatre?' asked Jack. 'I mean, if no one knows where the tunnel leads, we could get them to walk along it, then trap them in the theatre and force them to watch the performance!'

'Nice idea, but they stopped usin' the tunnel in the nineteen fifties. No one knows how strong it is, so it's not safe to go down anymore. Besides, could you really imagine all the old folk, not to mention Albie, walkin' down an unknown black hole?'

'No,' said Jack.

'Anyway, Becky, even though it's of no use to us now, I just wanted to show you the tunnel. What it says to me is that even though fifty years ago the Renegade Group took over Thistlewick and banned theatre, the Thistlewick Thespians were determined to keep it alive, and they managed to find ways of doin' it, like this here tunnel. So if they did all that to get one over on the Renegade Group, it shouldn't be too hard for us to find a way of gettin' people along to the theatre.'

CHAPTER 28

The Dress Rehearsal

Ted's news about the planned destruction of Midsummer House made everyone realise just how much they had left to do to get the production ready.

The date for the final performance had been set for September 3rd – the anniversary of Emily's disappearance from Thistlewick. This gave them only two weeks to prepare for it.

Becky was starting to panic. Most of the children had only just finished learning their lines; the set had a long way to go, with backdrops to be painted and props designed; lighting had to be organised and Cyril and Ted were trying their best to rig up the old lighting system, which was positioned in the balcony.

On top of it all, everyone was still worrying about how they were actually going to get people to come – not least

Becky. When Ted had shown her the secret tunnel it had given her confidence that they could find a way, but she was becoming more and more frustrated that she couldn't think of it.

The tension was showing in everyone as tempers started to flare. It all came to a head during the dress rehearsal three days before the production – the first time everyone had tried on their costumes, and the first time they'd run through the performance in full.

They had just come back from lunch.

'Ok, we're going to go from scene nine,' said Cyril. 'The Queen is awaiting Andrew's arrival.'

Becky waited on the stage. Her maid was meant to walk on and accidentally spill water over her.

'Issie, are you ready?' Cyril asked when she didn't appear. 'The scene's started.'

Suddenly a voice came from off stage. 'I'm fed up of this!'

Isabel stomped out of the wings and onto the stage, wearing her maid's dirty overalls.

'This costume is horrible.'

Becky, feeling more in character than she ever had done, with her long white robe, pearly shoes and pointy crown, stared menacingly at Isabel. Cyril had said that if anything went wrong they should just carry on, and make up lines if they had to. So this is what Becky decided to do.

'How dare you speak like that in the presence of your Queen!'

'Oh would you shut up. You're not a stupid Queen, this isn't real!'

'Take her away! I want her beheaded!'

'Arrg! I've had enough on this stupid play. I quit!'

Isabel let out a loud scream, stormed over to Becky and pushed over the new throne she was sitting on. Becky toppled backwards, her crown fell off and as she landed on top of it there was a snapping sound.

'Issie, come off the stage, now!' Cyril shouted. 'Are you alright, Becky?'

She looked up from where she lay and saw everyone staring at her. 'Fine. I think my crown's broken, though.'

After Isabel had calmed down and Cyril had had a chat with her, she eventually decided the production wasn't stupid and that she would carry on with it, as long as she could make her costume a bit more attractive.

As she walked past Becky she gave her a very icy 'Sorry.'

Cyril talked to everyone and emphasised that they needed to stick together and work as a team. This seemed to clear the air and they were able to carry on with the rehearsal.

***

That evening Becky lay on her bed, kicking her feet around in the air as she tried desperately to think of something that would get people to come along to the theatre in three days' time. It felt like the whole production was relying on her.

She had gone through lots of ideas that had led to dead ends, and now her mind was blank.

The house was almost in silence – all she could hear was the ticking of the clock from the hallway and the sound of her mum flicking through the pages of a book in her bedroom.

The sound of rustling paper gave Becky an idea. *I wonder if Emily says anything in her diary that can help.*

She took the red leather book out of her cupboard and started to flick through it, stopping at entries that she thought might give her advice.

She didn't know how long she had been doing this for, but it felt like hours by the time she reached the final entry, where Emily talked about her protest on Roden's Rock.

Roden's Rock. That's it! Roden's Rock!

Suddenly Becky had a brainwave. She read the entry.

...So on that morning, I made my way over to Roden's Rock, early enough to slip past the guards on the shoreline. I walked onto the rock and started to protest: I chose a scene from The Magic Paintbrush and acted it out for all to hear...

Roden's Rock appeared only once a year, for a few hours on September 1st. Over fifty years ago, Emily had chosen this occasion to protest. And it had worked – the Renegade Group had seen her and so had a lot of the islanders.

Becky looked over at the calendar on her wall. Today was August 31st, which meant that tomorrow Roden's Rock would appear once again.

CHAPTER 29
Roden's Rock

The rain came gently down as the sun fought its way through the cloudy sky. It was seven thirty in the morning by the time Becky had reached the entrance to Lower Farm.

Having sat up for most of the night thinking about what she was about to do, she had been very tired and slept through her alarm. Now, as she slipped past the farmhouse and down to the bay behind it, she was half an hour later than planned.

She approached the edge of the small cliff and heard the crash of the waves in front of her – the sea was rough this morning. Looking ahead, she couldn't miss it. Roden's Rock. A small, grey, dome-shaped mass rising out of the sea.

I hope this is going to work.

There were stepping-stones leading out to the rock, which dated from when it was used to drown witches hundreds of years ago. Each stone was carved into the shape of an animal – Becky could see the first two were a rabbit and a turtle. When the witches had taken the walk to their death, these stones were meant to have shown them the beauty of the world they were leaving behind. Roden's Rock itself was said to resemble the face of the devil, so that the witches knew the fate that awaited them as the waters rose, drowning their bodies and covering the rock up for another year.

Becky tried not to think of this as she placed her foot nervously on the first stepping-stone. It was slippery and she struggled to find a grip. She had never been good with water, and the previous year she'd come last in her school's swimming race.

There was quite a big gap between the first and second stone and the water rushed furiously between them. Becky would have to jump from one to the other.

Instead of thinking about the jump, she closed her eyes and tried to concentrate on what she was going to do when she reached Roden's Rock.

I will act as the Queen and show everyone on Thistlewick the power of theatre! If it worked for Emily, then I can do it too. I can show them why Midsummer House shouldn't be destroyed!

Becky opened her eyes and to her surprise found herself on the second, turtle-shaped stepping-stone.

A few minutes later she was scrambling up the side of Roden's Rock, gripping onto barnacles to help her climb to the top. She wobbled slightly as she stood up, but then gained her balance and took in a deep breath.

Looking back at Thistlewick, she could see Lower Farm to her left, Stormy Cliff School to her right and all the other buildings stretching out beyond them.

This is it.

She tried to focus on turning her fear of standing on the rock into the power of the Queen.

'I am the Queen of this land. Those who know me fear my presence. Those who serve me fear my power. And that is how it should be.'

When she had walked out to the rock, the world around her had seemed almost silent. Now, though, as she spoke, the sound of the wind rushing past her and the waves crashing against the rock overpowered her words. If she was struggling to hear what she was saying, how would anyone on the island hear her?

'If you cross me, or if you anger me, I will see that you are sentenced to death by beheading. Such is my power, and that is why I am feared by all in my kingdom!'

Looking over at the island, at the buildings spread out around the grassland, reality suddenly hit Becky.

What am I doing?

There was no one there! When Emily had held her protest there were guards from the Renegade Group who saw her and people walking to work on the farm. But there wasn't a living soul in sight to witness Becky's performance on Roden's Rock.

She stumbled forwards, her feet slipping on the wet rock, and fell over onto her front. All she could see as she lay there was the menacing water getting closer and closer, the waves splashing cold spray into her face and the sea starting to swallow Roden's Rock again.

Becky stood up and squinted back to the shore. To her horror, she saw that the stepping-stones – the only way of getting back to the island – had all but vanished. She was trapped!

She started to feel very dizzy and swayed heavily from side to side. Her vision became blurred and as she collapsed again she barely heard the voice calling out to her from the shoreline.

'Becky! What are you doing? Becky!'

***

'You're lucky your mum saw you,' said Ted. 'A few minutes later and I might not have been able to reach you.'

Becky sat shivering in the old fishing hut. Her hands were wrapped around a warm cup of tea, now diluted with her tears.

Her mum had been out on her early morning postal round and was delivering a parcel to Lower Farm when she saw Becky struggling out at sea. She had run to the harbour and alerted Ted, who had been the only fisherman there. Becky guessed he must have realised what she was trying to do. He had taken his boat out and sailed round to find her unconscious, lying on the remaining few feet of Roden's Rock.

'What on earth were you doing?' her mum asked. Her voice wasn't angry, though – it was soft. The sort of soft that told Becky her mum was worried about her.

'I… I was just trying to help. I thought it would work…' She was struggling to think straight.

'Becky, I don't understand.' Her mum sat down beside her.

'I think you need to tell your mum what's been goin' on,' said Ted, who was untangling a drift net in a corner of the hut.

Becky took in several deep breaths, forcing herself to focus properly. As she did, she felt a terrible pain in her heart. If she told her mum everything, it would mean the end of her dream. The theatre and all their hard work would be finished. But she felt so tired now, and there was no other excuse she could think of. Besides, if she didn't tell her mum, Ted would.

So she started at the beginning and worked her way slowly through the story of the Secret Theatre, as her vision kept slipping in and out of focus. When she eventually looked up at her mum, she couldn't read the expression on her face.

Becky expected her to be angry. She would shout, tell Becky she was lying. Eventually, though, her mum would realise it was the truth, and would tell Albert and the council what had been happening. That would be the end of the Secret Theatre.

What Becky definitely didn't expect, though, were the three words that came out of her mum's mouth.

'I'm sorry, Becky.'

'W… what?'

'I'm sorry for not believing you, about the theatre.' Her mum held out her arm and Becky cuddled into it. 'I trusted the island council more than my own daughter. But you wouldn't have put yourself through what you just did for nothing.'

'So you're not angry?'

'No, love. After what you've just told me, I don't care if theatre is banned. It's something you believe in, so I'm happy to support you.'

'Thanks, Mum.'

'We're going to have to look after you, Becky Evans.' Her mum squeezed her tightly. 'So, are you going to show me the Secret Theatre?'

***

Becky tucked into her fish and chips eagerly that evening.

After they had gone to the theatre in the morning, her mum had taken her back home and she had fallen straight

172

to sleep on the sofa. When she awoke, she had found herself lying in bed, thirsty and starving. It was six o'clock in the evening.

'If there's any way I can help with the theatre, Becky, do tell me,' her mum said from across the table.

'She needs mental help that one, standing on Roden's Rock in that weather,' said William.

'Yes… well I'm sure there are more effective ways to get people's attention,' said her mum.

Becky thought for a while as she turned a chip around on her fork.

'Mum, could you deliver an advert to all the houses you go to on your postal round tomorrow morning?'

She knew they had all agreed this wasn't a good idea, but with only a day and a half to go until the performance, it was worth a try. They could miss out the houses of all the council members.

'Sorry, love, that would be against post office regulations.'

'Couldn't you just ignore them this one time?'

'No, Becky, I'm afraid it's out of the question.'

Becky dropped her knife and fork on her plate and stood up.

'And you said you'd help!'

She stormed out of the room before her mum had a chance to reply.

CHAPTER 30
Trapped!

'Our final day.'

Becky was sitting on the stage at the Secret Theatre reading Emily's diary. It was eight o'clock in the morning and the rest of the New Thistlewick Thespians were starting to get everything ready for the final performance.

William and Jimmy were practising their lines together on stage; a group of the girls were putting finishing touches to their costumes, hanging them on the ladder that Cyril was halfway up, still trying to sort out the lights. Jack was going back and forth, bringing in props from the entrance hall, while Ted and some of the other boys were painting a backdrop of trees, for Andrew's journey through the dark forest.

A tapping sound started to come from the roof and everyone stopped to listen. It began quite softly and then got louder and faster.

'It's raining,' said William.

'Sounds like people clapping,' said Ben.

'Maybe the only applause we'll get tonight is from the rain,' Becky said.

'Come on, Becky. What would Emily say?' asked Cyril.

'Be positive.'

'Exactly. This is the day that Emily never got, the day that we have the chance to bring theatre back to Thistlewick. And that's all thanks to you, Becky.'

'But what if we fail? What if no one turns up?

'Even if you end up only performing to Ted, your mum and me, it will still be an achievement,' said Cyril.

'And what if people do turn up? We might be no good. And… and what if Albert tries to stop us?'

'You aren't just good, you're all superb,' said Cyril. 'And even if Albert does try to stop us, would you have missed any of what has happened these past few weeks?'

Becky thought back to when she'd discovered the Secret Theatre; to everything she had learnt from Emily in the diary; to the transformation of Cyril from an empty old man to someone with something to live for again. Then there were all the rehearsals with her friends, and of course the joy of acting.

She smiled. 'No, not for the world.'

'Right then,' Cyril said to everyone in the theatre. 'I think we can all agree, it's been a success whatever the outcome, because *we* know how amazing theatre is, and if no one else does, then so what? Tonight you just have to go out there and give the performance of your lives.'

There was a sudden, spontaneous cheer and everyone started to jump around in excitement.

By ten o'clock everything was in place, apart from the backdrops, which Ted and Jack were still painting. The rest of the New Thistlewick Thespians left them there to finish off.

'Ok, everyone,' said Cyril. 'You all need to go and relax for the rest of the day. I'll see if I can encourage a few of the islanders to come along tonight, but all you need to think about is the performance. We'll meet back at the theatre at five o'clock.'

* * *

'Come on, Jimmy, put some effort in.' Becky waved a script in front of him.

'Cyril said we should relax, Becky.'

'But what if we forget our lines?'

'That's not going to happen. You've known your lines for weeks.'

'I suppose. Want some chocolate?'

'Yes please.'

Becky opened up her secret drawer and took half a bar out. She opened it up on her bed and shared it between Jimmy and herself. Five pieces each.

'I haven't forced you into doing this, have I?' she asked.

'What do you mean?' asked Jimmy, his mouth full of chocolate.

'The production. You didn't want to do it because of not telling your mum.'

'No, Becky, you didn't force me. I'm really looking forward to the performance tonight, and I've learnt a lot doing the production.'

'You've grown, and you're more confident.'

Jimmy grinned.

The front door suddenly slammed and a sound like a charging elephant reverberated around the walls as someone raced up the stairs. Becky's door burst open and William came through, out of breath.

'What's up?' she asked.

'Bad news, Becky. There are diggers. On Thistlewick. Diggers and bulldozers. They're coming in from the harbour and heading towards Midsummer House!'

'Oh no, it's happening!' Becky couldn't believe it. 'But Ted said they wouldn't try to destroy Midsummer House for at least a month!'

'Well they are, and they've blocked the front door. No one can get in or out.'

'What? But there are people in there!'

'Jack and Ted!' William said in realisation.

'What can we do?' asked Becky. 'They're trapped and they don't even know it! They'll be killed!'

'You stay here,' said William. 'I've got to go and get Cyril. We'll see what he says.'

'No way! We can't stay here. We have to warn Ted.'

'Fine, you go to Midsummer House, but I don't see how you're going to persuade them to unblock the door.'

'The tunnel! We can use the tunnel to get to the theatre!'

'What tunnel?' asked William.

'I thought you said the tunnel was dangerous?' said Jimmy.

'Look, I have to go,' said William. He turned away, but before he left he glanced back at Becky. 'Just don't do anything stupid. Mum will never forgive me if something happens to you. I'll see you at Midsummer House.'

In a flash he was gone.

'Come on. We need coats and a torch. There's one in the post office, I think. I'll get that and meet you outside.'

'But…'

'There's no time for buts, Jimmy. People are in danger. We have to save them!'

Chapter 31

Down the Tunnel

'*Arrg!* Why is no one answering!'

Becky banged on the Castles' front door again, harder.

'We don't have time for this. Is the shed definitely locked, Jimmy?'

'Yep,' said Jimmy, standing by the boat shed. 'This rusty old padlock won't budge and there isn't a key anywhere.'

'Ok. Move out of the way.'

'What?'

'Move away from the shed.'

As Jimmy stepped backwards, Becky ran towards the shed door and took a flying kick at it. It didn't burst open like she'd hoped, but she managed to knock a large hole in it.

'Help me make the hole bigger.'

Together they tore away at the old wood. It came out easily and soon Becky was able to fit through. She grabbed Jimmy's hand and pulled him into the shed.

'Torch.'

Jimmy handed her the pen torch she had found in a drawer in the post office. She turned it on and in its dim light they could just see to the end of the shed. The trap door was still uncovered.

They ran over and managed to lift it up between them.

'Right, are you ready?' asked Becky.

'No.'

'Come on then.'

She jumped down into the hole. The drop was further than she had thought and she landed painfully on her back. There was a loud crack.

'Are you alright?' called Jimmy.

'Yes. That wasn't me.' She shone the torch on the ground around her. 'I think I've just landed in a fish graveyard.'

There were lots of small skeletons around her. Various fish must have fallen down over the years from the nets that rested in the boat shed above. It wasn't a pleasant sight.

Becky stood up and cleared a space on the ground with her foot for Jimmy to land in.

'Come on.'

Somehow, he managed to position himself over the hole and was about to jump. But then he started to climb nimbly down the wall.

'How are you doing that?' asked Becky.

'There's a ladder,' replied Jimmy.

'Oh.'

He jumped the last few feet and landed beside her. They started to walk forwards into the gloom.

Shining the torch around, Becky saw that the walls were made up of rough, damp granite. The ceiling of the tunnel wasn't very high and if they'd been adults, they would have had to bend over in order to fit in. Occasionally a wooden beam stretched across between the walls. How wood was supposed to hold up rock Becky didn't know, but she just had to hope that she and Jimmy would be safe.

The tunnel was also very wide.

'They would have needed this space to take all the pieces of the theatre along here,' she told Jimmy. He remained silent. 'You ok?'

'Yes.' His voice was very quiet.

She held her hand out to him and he took it gladly. They carried on, scurrying further into the darkness.

Minutes seemed to turn into hours and Becky had no idea how long they had been in the tunnel. She didn't even know how far it was from Ted's cottage to Midsummer House using this route. The tunnel was quite straight, and she guessed it would be about a mile and a half long, because that was the distance it was when travelling over ground.

Jimmy seemed to be having similar thoughts. 'I wonder what's above us now.'

'I think we're under the market.'

It was a complete guess, and Becky could hear nothing from the world above to confirm it, but she tried to convince herself they were directly under her mum, busy at work in the post office. If Becky was right, it meant they were almost halfway to their destination.

As the tunnel went on, Becky started to notice fragments of rock scattered on the ground. The rocks got bigger and more frequent as they progressed.

'Do you think we could run?' she asked after a while. 'We need to get there as soon as possible.'

'We could try,' said Jimmy uncertainly.

'Come on then. I'll race you.'

She shot off, leaving her friend behind. She ran quickly, using the torch to help her avoid the large rocks scattered on the ground. Jimmy's footsteps echoed through the tunnel behind her. After a minute or so she stopped to catch her breath.

'Oooww!'

It was Jimmy. His footsteps had suddenly stopped. With a pang of guilt, Becky realised he didn't have a torch. While she was charging around using the torch to guide her, he was running blind.

'Are you ok, Jimmy?'

She walked back, shining the torch down the tunnel, until she found her friend. He was kneeling on the ground rubbing his head.

'I hit my head on that beam,' he said.

'Oh. I'm really sorry, Jimmy, I shouldn't have left you.'

She glanced up above her. There was a big crack along the centre of the rotten wooden beam.

'You must have a hard head. Look at the crack you've made!'

A small rumble came from the ceiling.

'What was that?' asked Jimmy.

But Becky didn't have time to reply. In a split second, the beam fell. Becky dived to the ground as the wood came crashing down between her and Jimmy.

The rumbling sound got louder, and with a horrible feeling Becky realised what was happening.

'Jimmy, you need to move. Carefully, towards me.'

Jimmy took his hand off his head and stared at her, puzzled. Then he followed her gaze upwards.

The ceiling started to crumble above them, small fragments of rock coming down like thick black rain. Then, in an instant, large chunks of rock started to fall around them.

'Forget being careful, Jimmy, run!'

Becky grabbed hold of him and pulled him through the falling rock with all her might. They charged off as fast as they could as the sound that rang around the tunnel deafened them.

Glancing back briefly, Becky saw that the tunnel was completely blocked off by fallen rocks. There was no way of getting back!

'What do we do?' asked Jimmy.

'We keep going.'

'Becky, I'm scared.'

She stopped running and stood still, but it felt like her heart had continued along the tunnel, it was racing so fast. She couldn't show she was scared, though – that would just make things worse. She thought desperately for a way she could help Jimmy.

'How would Andrew feel?' she asked.

'What do you mean? Andrew?' His voice was shaking badly, and he obviously wasn't thinking straight.

'Your character in the play. How would he feel if he was in our position?'

'He'd be... confident, I guess. Determined.'

'Right, so act as Andrew.'

'I can't.'

'Don't speak to your Queen like that!' she shouted. 'You must guide me to safety. There's no room for cowards in my kingdom.'

It seemed to work. Jimmy bowed to her and started to walk forwards.

'Follow me, your majesty.'

He started to whistle, like Andrew did as he entered the forest in the play. Whenever he was scared, he whistled, and it helped him to control his nerves.

Being the Queen helped Becky too. She was so glad that Cyril had taught her how to turn her fear into the Queen's power. It had helped her to conquer her stage fright, it had saved her on Roden's Rock, and now it would help her get to the end of the tunnel.

***

A small, faint light appeared ahead of them. Eagle-eyed, they started to walk quickly towards it

'Can you hear that, your majesty?'

'Is it the sound of hammering?'

'Yes, your majesty.'

'Then move on, with haste.'

Becky looked at Jimmy and they both grinned. They had reached the end of the tunnel!

Breaking out of character, they ran towards the noise.

Above them, there were thin gaps in the ceiling, the light shining through to make a square shape.

'It's another trap door,' Becky said. 'We must be under the stage. That's where Ted said the tunnel comes out.'

The banging noise was coming from directly above them.

'Help!' they shouted together.

'We're down here!' called Becky. 'Help!'

'D'you hear that?' came Jack's voice from directly above them. 'There's a noise coming from under here, Dad.'

'The trap door!' exclaimed Ted.

They heard footsteps echoing along towards them.

'Hello?'

'Help! It's Becky and Jimmy!'

There was a long pause, followed by footsteps walking away from them.

'Don't leave us!' called Becky.

A few seconds later, the footsteps returned and there was a loud scraping noise above them as a metal pole descended through one of the gaps.

'Becky, Jimmy, move away from the trap door. I'm goin' to lever it up with the pole,' came Ted's voice.

Four tugs of the pole later, the trap door swung open and Ted and Jack helped Becky and Jimmy to climb out.

'What on earth were you—?' Ted began.

'They're going to destroy Midsummer House today! There are bulldozers coming and they've blocked the front door!'

As Becky spoke, an eerie humming sound started somewhere around them – the sound of machinery.

'We have to get out,' said Ted. 'The tunnel, is it safe?'

'No, it collapsed behind us.'

'We'll have to go to the front door, then. Let's hope someone's there to let us out!'

CHAPTER 32
Albert

All four of them pushed against the door with all their might.

'It's not going to budge,' said Ted, a note of panic in his voice.

Becky pressed her ear to the door. The constant hum of the machinery immediately became louder, but she could also hear voices nearby.

'…but there are people in there!' Cyril was shouting.

'There's not a livin' soul in Midsummer House. We've barricaded the door to stop people gettin' in,' Albert replied.

'Why won't you listen to me?'

'This is no time to get angry, Cyril.'

'Why doesn't Cyril just tell Albert the truth about what we've been doing?' asked Jack.

'Are you all ready to make a lot of noise?' said Ted. 'Our only hope of gettin' out now is if someone hears us.'

Becky started to scream at the top of her voice and the others followed her lead. They all banged as hard as they could on the front door.

'Did you hear that?' said Cyril. 'No... no, Albert, I'm serious. Listen.'

They all shouted again and doubled their rate of banging.

'Clear the door! Clear the door! There are people in there!' called Albert.

For several minutes, Becky heard banging and clattering on the other side of the door. Then the handle turned and the door swung open, casting bright sunlight into the entrance hall.

'Thank goodness,' said Cyril from in front of them.

'Ted!' said Albert.

'Hello, Albie.'

Becky had never before seen anyone as shocked as Albert was now. She didn't even see his wrinkles, or his straggly beard – all she saw was an image of shock. Then, looking past him, she saw a sight that gave her an expression to match Albert's.

'Look at all the people,' said Jimmy from beside her.

Standing around the perimeter of Midsummer House and stretching out into the distance were hundreds of Thistlewickians. At the front of them, Becky saw her mum. She ran over to her.

'What's happening?' she asked.

Everything was a blur. All the people seemed to be staring in one direction, to the right side of Midsummer House. Becky turned around to see a great monster of a machine being driven up to it. A bulldozer, at least half the size of the house and glaring a menacing red colour. Behind it was another machine, which had a huge black ball swinging in front of it.

She turned back to look at the mass of people, and then at her mum.

'Why are all these people here?' she asked.

'It seems someone tipped them all off about the destruction of Midsummer House,' said Cyril, standing beside Becky. He turned his head towards her mum.

'I saw all the machines being unloaded at the harbour when I was on my late morning rounds,' her mum said. 'I knew what was going on, so I started knocking on people's doors and telling them about it – there was bound to be interest, great big machines like those on Thistlewick. No one believed me, but then they heard the sound of the machines roaring past the houses. Word gets around quickly, and everyone flooded here to see it all.' She looked at her daughter affectionately. 'It's not ideal, Becky, but this is your only chance. You've got the whole island here, at the theatre. Now's the time to show them.'

Becky smiled at her mum and gave her a big hug.

Then she turned around and saw Albert and Ted arguing heatedly near the house. The crowd's attention seemed to be on the bulldozer. She knew what she had to do.

She ran as fast as she could back through the front door and into the entrance hall of Midsummer House, only just hearing her mum shouting, 'Becky, what are you doing?' and Ted calling Albert a 'stubborn old fool'.

In the toilet Becky lifted up the picture of the Globe, pulled the lever and flushed the toilet. The costume cupboard appeared and at the front was the Queen's costume.

She hurriedly put it on.

This hadn't worked on Roden's Rock, but now she knew it would. Becky had an audience and she was ready to perform.

Breathing in deeply, feeling the harsh material of the gown against her skin, she became the Queen. She stepped out of the cupboard and back into the entrance hall. Through the darkness, golden light shimmered around the front door, like the light at the end of a tunnel.

If what she was about to do worked, Becky knew they would have a chance. If it didn't, it would mean the death of the theatre and all her dreams.

She ran out through the door and straight into the crowd. She could hear the cries of people around her, but they were muffled, as if Becky was surrounded by an invisible wall. Looking around frantically, she tried to find the highest point. Her eyes came to the bulldozer.

It felt like it was all happening in slow motion. Becky ran towards it, and was faintly aware of men in yellow jackets trying to stop her. Their hands barely touched her as she made a flying leap for the front of the machine. As she hit it heavily, reality suddenly came back into being.

Becky heard the cries of the crowd behind her, and gruff voices close by.

'What's she doing?'

'Get down, girl!'

She scrambled up onto the front of the bulldozer and, gripping the open side door, positioned herself on the front of the machine. As she turned around to face the crowd, she felt the sun hit her back and her audience was lit up powerfully. It was the wrong way round – everyone around her with the light shining on them while she was in darkness. But it didn't matter – she started to perform.

'I am the Queen of your kingdom. You will all follow my rule. And if you don't, you will face the blade of my finest axe-man.'

As she continued to perform, she heard murmurs from below her.

'Who is that up there?'

'What's she saying?'

She saw Albert breaking away from his argument with Ted and turning around.

'It's... it's Emily!' he exclaimed. 'Back to finish Renegade's work!'

'That's not Emily, it's young Becky,' called the vicar.

'What on earth is she doing up there?' asked Sergeant Radley.

'She's acting!' said Harriet.

'She's what?!' cried Albert.

'What a big crowd has come to see me paint!'

Everyone's attention moved away from Becky at the sound of this new voice. Squinting down, Becky saw Jimmy striding out below her and addressing the crowd. 'My name is Andrew and I am an eleven-year-old artist.'

He showed them his magic paintbrush and explained what the play was about.

'So,' Becky called out, 'if you want to find out what happens to Andrew, and whether I, the Queen, behead him or not, you must come with us into Midsummer House and the Secret Theatre, where we will perform the story of *The Magic Paintbrush*!'

As she climbed down from the bulldozer, the crowd around her exploded into a thousand voices as everyone talked excitedly to each other. Jimmy helped her down and together they walked to the entrance of Midsummer House.

Her heart in her mouth, Becky looked back at the islanders behind her.

'Will this work?' she whispered to Jimmy.

'Only one way of finding out,' he said.

'Follow us!' they called.

Remarkably, people started to walk towards them. At first it was only Cyril, Ted and their fellow Thespians. But others followed and soon a large line of people was queuing up outside Midsummer House.

Then a voice came over the top of everyone. 'No! Stop!'

It was Albert.

Everything went silent as he ran to the front, standing between the crowd and Becky and Jimmy, who were in the doorway.

'You must not go in! What they are doin' is wrong. Theatre is banned!' His voice was loud and carried clearly around the gathered islanders.

'Albert, you can't keep blaming the Thespians for the past,' said Cyril.

'But they betrayed us. Emily Wilson betrayed us and she dragged Ralph Little with her. He would never have gone if Emily and her theatre hadn't influenced him.'

'That's not true, Albert!' Becky shouted.

'I don't believe you,' Albert replied.

'Then believe *me*.'

Becky looked past Albert, trying to see where the new voice had come from. Her mum stepped forwards and everyone turned to face her.

'I have someone to introduce to you,' she said.

From behind her a man stepped out. He would have been quite tall if it wasn't for his stoop, and he looked old, almost as old as Albert.

'R... Ralph?' Albert stuttered.

Becky looked at the man again in amazement – was this Ralph Little, the man who was said to have betrayed Thistlewick?

Cyril seemed equally amazed to see the former Thespian. 'How... how did you find him?' he asked Becky's mum.

'There was still a few details about him in the post office records. I recognised the name two nights ago and managed to track him down. I thought the best way to solve all this would be to bring Ralph over himself.'

She smiled at Becky, and Becky grinned back – her mum had helped after all.

'Albie, I'm here to tell you that Emily didn't betray you,' said Ralph. 'I did, I admit that, and I will regret it forever. But Emily had strength. She fought Renegade. When she was seen leaving Thistlewick, it was because Renegade had captured her and was taking her away.'

'What happened to her?' Becky asked.

'I don't know. We went on the same boat. But when we reached land, I went one way with Renegade and she was taken the other. I'm sad to say I never saw her again. But believe me, Albie, she didn't betray you.'

'But *you* did!' Albert said.

'Yes. And please let me explain why.' Ralph walked a few steps closer, but Albert stood his ground. 'My mother,

Albie, you remember her? She was bedridden and dying. There was no way I could save her without medicine, but Renegade wouldn't let me have any. Her condition worsened, and I became so desperate that I struck a bargain with him. I joined the Renegade Group so that she could have medicine.'

There was a loud murmur around the collection of people closest to Midsummer House as Ralph revealed the truth about the past.

'Did… did you ever think of comin' back?' said Albert, his voice shaking.

'How could I? I felt so ashamed of what I'd done. I lived out a life of misery serving Renegade, and I never saw my family again. I know my mother survived her illness, though, so it wasn't for nothing,' said Ralph.

'But she was heartbroken for the rest of her life. She missed you.'

Ralph closed his eyes and gritted his teeth. Becky could tell he was holding back a lot of emotion. Cyril walked over to him and gave him a warm hug.

'Thank you, Cyril,' Ralph finally said. 'That's all in the past now, Albie. What I can see in the present, though, is a young girl who's put a lot of effort into bringing theatre back to Thistlewick.' He smiled at Becky. 'Now you know that theatre wasn't the reason for my betrayal, can you please let this production go ahead?'

Becky saw a tear trickle down Albert's cheek. She felt a strange mixture of feelings towards him now. She could understand his shock, and felt so sorry that he had found out about Ralph this way. But she also couldn't help but be angry with him as well. He was the only person stopping the theatre now.

'I... I don't know what to think,' he said.

'Well I think we should see this production,' said the vicar.

'Hear, hear!' said Mrs Didsbury. There was a lot of agreement from people around them.

But Becky could see that Albert was still confused.

'How... how can I believe... I don't know if I can... after all this time...'

'How about this, Albie,' said Ted. 'Let's make a deal. Come in and watch the production. If you don't like it, by all means have those bulldozers destroy Midsummer House and wash all your memories of the past away. But if you do enjoy what you see, lift the ban of theatre on Thistlewick.'

There was a long pause. Becky's heart missed several beats. Then Albert said one word.

'Ok.'

Chapter 33

The Final Performance?

Becky paced up and down behind the curtain, listening to the sounds coming from the other side; she felt very nervous now about Ted's deal with Albert. Everyone else was sorting out their costumes around her with Cyril and Ted helping. Becky's mum was organising the seating of the audience.

'Right, gather round, everyone,' said Cyril.

They all shuffled over to him and formed a tight group. Becky made her way to the front.

'We don't have much time. Everyone is taking their seats and our performance will begin soon. We must remember that although we've succeeded in getting everyone here, our fight is far from over. In fact it has just begun. We must prove that what we're doing is right, that theatre is a great thing, and that it should have a special place here on Thistlewick. If we don't, then there are machines outside waiting to destroy Midsummer House. But that's not going to happen. I have complete confidence in every one of you. Together, as the New Thistlewick Thespians, we can do this!'

Everyone let out a loud cheer and Becky felt an excited buzz around her as they all moved off to continue their preparations. She wished she could feel excited too, but she couldn't settle and continued to pace around.

Ted headed over towards the curtain.

'Where are you going, Ted?' she asked.

'I'm off to man the lights up in the balcony, Becky. Cyril'll be backstage to help you.'

'Where is Albert sitting?' she asked.

'We thought we'd put him in the front row. Give him the best view possible. Anyway, I must get goin' or we won't have any lights. Good luck, Becky – or as they say in the theatre, break a leg!'

'Thanks, Ted.'

He moved out through the curtains. As he went, they flapped briefly and Becky saw through into the stalls. They were already about half full and the whole theatre suddenly seemed much bigger with so many people in it. She could feel a buzz coming from them, and just hoped it was an excited buzz like the one backstage. She saw her mum standing in the central isle, smiling at Mrs Didsbury as she directed her to a seat. Albert wasn't anywhere in the front row – he obviously hadn't been given his seat yet.

She turned around and looked at all her friends. Jimmy was already in costume and talking with Cyril while William was sitting next to them reading through his script. Jack was busy putting props out on the stage for the first scene – Andrew's discovery of the magic paintbrush.

Becky thought about what she had read in Emily's diary the night before.

Close your eyes and imagine the whole audience cheering for you at the end, as if you've given the best performance the world has ever seen!

Becky closed her eyes and tried to see everyone standing up in their seats applauding as she took a bow. But all she could see was Albert, standing high above her, his face replaced by a cruel golden mask from her last nightmare. She shook her head, trying to remove the image from her mind. It wouldn't budge. She opened her eyes.

'Be confident! You can do this,' she said to herself.

She closed her eyes again, and this time she saw the whole audience erupting in front of her. Mrs Didsbury was clapping; Sergeant Radley was chuckling merrily; her mum was beaming with pride. Everyone loved it!

As she opened her eyes, Becky saw Cyril standing next to her.

'Two minutes, everyone! Starting positions,' he called; then he bent down beside her and whispered, 'This is for Emily.'

Becky nodded, and suddenly felt more determined. She moved over to a seat backstage, next to where Isabel was sitting. They watched as Jimmy walked onto the stage.

There was a moment of complete silence.

The curtains opened; light shone over Jimmy.

The final performance had begun.

***

Scene one wasn't long, but to Becky it felt like it lasted for hours. She realised she didn't have a clue how the performance was going. She could hear Jimmy well enough, and he sounded great, but from backstage she couldn't see what was happening or how the audience was reacting. She just had to hope.

As the scene ended, Jimmy walked off into the right wing and Becky heard the sound of clapping.

'They like it!' said Cyril.

Jimmy walked over to sit beside Becky.

'Well done,' she whispered to him. 'How was it?'

'Amazing!' he replied with a big grin. 'Just… amazing. Those lights are so powerful that the stage could probably been seen from space if the theatre didn't have a roof.'

'How does Albert look?'

'Uncomfortable.'

'Becky,' someone whispered from her other side. She turned around to see Jack. 'You need to get ready for scene three. You're on in two minutes.'

She waited by the side of the stage as Jack moved her throne into position during the blackout between scenes two and three. There wasn't time to feel nervous now – she knew what she had to do. Jack signalled that everything was ready and she went and sat down, staring out into the audience menacingly.

Even though she was 'in character' on the outside, on the inside she couldn't help but think about the people in front of her. She could hardly see them in the darkness, and this wasn't helped when the bright lights came up on the stage and blinded her. Scanning along the faces in the front row, she found Albert on her right hand side. He was sitting very upright at the edge of his seat, his hands clenched in fists, his face very tense.

To his left sat Ralph, but on Albert's right was an empty seat.

Becky's eyes soon became better adjusted to the light and she could see the audience more clearly. She glanced around them – the seat next to Albert was the only empty one in the whole theatre. Most of the island had come to see them perform!

Becky heard a small cough beside her and saw Isabel standing there, holding out a rather bad painting.

She grabbed hold of the painting, took one look at it and then snapped it in half over her knee.

Isabel looked at her with genuine fear in her eyes – they both knew that that wasn't in the script. But Becky felt more powerful than ever! She stood up and shouted.

'That was a feeble painting! How dare you show me such rubbish! Have the painter beheaded.'

As the words came out of her mouth, inside she finally felt a huge rush of excitement – her moment had arrived. Isabel ran off stage and Becky turned to Jack behind her.

'Take this and burn it!'

She threw the painting at her servant and stormed off stage.

Backstage, she punched the air with joy and relief as she heard the audience clapping.

The performance continued and before Becky knew it, act one drew to a close with Andrew's magic paintbrush being stolen in the forest when he was on his way to paint the Queen.

***

Halfway through the interval, Ted reappeared backstage.

'You're all doing really well. I'm hearin' some great comments out there.'

'Has Albert said anything yet?' Cyril asked quietly.

Becky moved closer to hear Ted's reply.

'Not a word,' he said. He forced a smile onto his face. 'Keep it up, everyone!'

Cyril turned to Becky. 'So, the second act is your big moment. Are you ready?'

'Definitely. I can't wait. Everything Emily said about acting is true, isn't it?'

'Oh yes. You never know what a brilliant feeling acting gives you until you experience performing in front of an audience. So go out there and give them everything you've got!'

'I will.'

'And Becky, I'm really proud of you.'

'Thank you.'

'Everyone in positions for act two!' called Jack.

***

As act two started, Andrew arrived at the Queen's castle. Without his paintbrush he wouldn't be able to paint, and the Queen would behead him. Then he met Philip, an artist played by William, who was doing a painting of the castle. Philip also had a magic paintbrush and lent it to Andrew. They entered the castle together.

As she stepped onto the stage for her next scene, Becky couldn't help but think back to the time she had got stage fright weeks before in front of only fifteen people. How scared she would have been in front of the hundreds she stood before now.

'Ah, so you are the painter. Much younger than I expected, but still the same rules apply. Paint me well and you will be rich, paint me poorly and you die.'

She felt so in character that she didn't see the audience at all. She didn't really notice Jimmy's brilliant performance or William's perfect reactions; she saw only Andrew and Philip, trembling in the presence of their Queen.

The only chance she had to look out into the audience was halfway through scene twelve, when she had to sit still as Andrew painted her. Looking around, she saw many faces fixed on the stage. Her eyes moved straight to Albert.

He was sitting back in his chair, his hands lay forgotten on the arm rests and he had an expression on his face that Becky remembered from somewhere.

It's the same one that little Bethie had when she saw her first play.

She thought back to her trip to the Theatre Royal, where she had met Henry Smith and his five-year-old granddaughter. As Bethie had followed every movement of each character, the look on her face had been one of such wide-eyed awe and fascination that it looked liked she'd wanted to jump onto the stage and be with the characters. That was the expression on Albert's face now.

Becky felt a tingle run around her body. She wanted to jump up in excitement.

You still have half a scene to get through, she reminded herself.

She released her excitement instead by shouting for her jester to entertain her.

***

As she ran off the stage at the end of the long scene, she flew straight into Cyril.

'We've done it! I think we've actually done it!'

Cyril looked at her, slightly puzzled.

'It's Albert, I think he's enjoying it!'

'Becky, that's fantastic!'

They shared a big grin, and it stayed with Becky all the way through the final scene, as she watched from the wing.

Andrew had successfully painted a portrait the Queen liked and was given a huge bag of gold by her

servant. He thanked Philip for the use of his magic paintbrush, and asked what made it magic.

'The secret of my magic paintbrush is that there is nothing magic about it at all,' said Philip. 'It's just an ordinary old paintbrush. You were the one who had the talent to paint the Queen, Andrew. All you needed was the confidence.'

As the curtains closed at the end to the sound of the audience's applause, Jimmy walked off the stage and Becky skipped over to him.

'Well done! You were amazing!' she said, giving him a big hug.

'So were you, Becky,' he replied.

'Did you see Albert?'

'Yes!'

'Ah…' said Cyril. 'We've forgotten something.'

Becky turned around to face him. 'What?'

'The curtain call, where everyone takes their bow. We've never practised it.'

'We'll do it together. One big bow,' Becky said.

Cyril nodded. 'Yes. Jack, gather everyone together, you're all going on for a bow.'

'That includes you,' Becky said. 'You're coming on too, Cyril.'

'But I haven't done anything. You're the ones who have put in all the hard work.'

'Cyril, you were our director. None of this would ever have happened without you.'

'We're all ready,' said Jack.

***

As the whole cast of *The Magic Paintbrush* came to the front of the stage and took their final bow to the cheering audience, Becky's mind was racing. The theatre wouldn't be destroyed now – it was safe!

She looked to the grey-haired old man standing beside her. But as a huge smile stretched over Cyril's face, Becky didn't see him as old any more; he was the little boy in the photo from years before, his eyes lit up in excitement.

Glancing around, she saw both Jimmy's mum and her own standing up and clapping along with everyone else. Becky could have sworn there was also a tear running down her mum's cheek. Then there was Albert, with a beaming smile on his face, clapping merrily and shaking Ralph's hand.

On Albert's other side, in the seat that had previously been the only empty one in the whole theatre, Becky saw a woman.

Emily Wilson's eyes were far brighter than in any of the photos Becky had seen of her, and she was smiling happily and proudly.

Becky looked to Cyril again. He was overwhelmed by the continuing applause.

'We've done Emily proud!' he said, with tears in his eyes. 'We have done her proud.'

Becky turned back to Emily, and watched as she slowly and peacefully faded away. Then tears of joy began to trickle down Becky's face as well.

'Yes,' she said. 'Yes we have.'

About the Author

Luke Temple was born in 1988. There are some quite surprising things about him:

When he was a child, for example, all Luke's school reports commented on what a delight he was to teach, but how poor his spelling was (it hasn't improved much since). Luke didn't enjoy reading when he was younger – and yet now he's an author.

He also didn't like standing up in front of lots of people – but now he regularly performs to hundreds of children at a time during his school visits.

Until the age of 13, Luke lived as an only child in the schools his parents taught at, and had great fun running around the grounds and making up his own adventures. It was the perfect preparation for a career in writing for children!

He's always enjoyed being creative: writing, drawing, painting, making films. He used to be able to sing, but anyone who's witnessed one of his school visits will know this is now not the case. These days he feels most at home in the world of books and storytelling.

When not behind his desk with his writing partners, a one-eyed dog called Sparky and a bald hamster called Cosmo, Luke spends most of his time visiting schools and bringing his stories to life with the children he meets. For him, this is the best part of his job.

He looks forward to writing more books in the 'Thistlewick Island' series and continuing on his author-adventure!

The Websites

If you'd like to find more about the 'Thistlewick Island' series and how Luke Temple writes it, visit:

www.thistlewick.net

There you can explore Thistlewick on an interactive map, find out more about the characters and the author, sign up to receive the Chronicles of Thistlewick Newsletter and much more!

In the 'The Secret Theatre' section you can create your own creepy theatre mask, find out just how the illustrations for the book were created and discover fun and spooky tales about theatre that inspired Luke to write the book.

There may also be a few secret pages to uncover along the way…

Teachers – find out about Luke Temple's exciting school visits at:

www.luketemple.co.uk

Luke is one of the youngest and most exciting authors visiting schools in the UK. He aims to bring writing to life with every child he meets during his school visits.

With a vibrant mix of interactive drama, singing, humour and much more he takes children on a journey to discover how he creates his books. There isn't a moment during a visit from Luke that children aren't fully involved, and by the end of the day many will be eager to read his books and have a go at writing their own stories.

To find out more and read testimonials from teachers and children, visit **www.luketemple.co.uk**

Acknowledgements

It is my passion for theatre that undoubtedly gave me the idea to write 'The Secret Theatre'.

I first found this passion while I was making films at secondary school. I thank my dedicated and caring tutor, Phil Cole, for introducing me to filmmaking, then encouraging me along with everyone else at Downlands. Phil soon showed me the concept of using film sequences as part of school plays.

I grabbed hold of this concept and developed it further, becoming involved in many more plays with directors Mike Temple and Cosmo Goldsmith, who I thank for allowing me far too much freedom. Each new play I worked on with them became the highlight of my year. Of course, none of these experiences would have been possible without my fellow projectioneer, Kieran Burling, to whom I owe a lot.

In recent years, my experiences at many theatres have helped to feed my passion, none more so than at the Theatre Royal Brighton. My visits there provided some of the inspiration for this book.

To my parents, I owe so much that I can't sum it up here. Without their commitment and support I wouldn't be writing these words now.

All my grandparents are special to me, but one character in this book is inspired by my Grandpa, Cyril Temple. Seeing him slowly grow frail when I was a child was heartbreaking, but I'll always remember his smile, and hopefully I have gone some of the way to bringing it back with this book.

Finally, I thank Jessica Chiba for allowing her wonderful talents to be associated with the 'Thistlewick Island' series. Without her fine artwork and font this book wouldn't be the same.

With love,
Luke